The Face I

Boo

Zoe Vlamaki

Dedication:

To those who live in mystery of unknown roots and inheritance.

Description:

The Face I Saw Once,

is a haunting journey through memory, mystery, and the labyrinth of human existence. When a forgotten photograph and a whispered secret draw a woman into a hidden world beneath Prague's streets, she must confront shadows from the past — and the fragile light of hope for the future.

Bound by a thread of family, fear, and forgotten identities, she steps into a maze where every corner hides a truth, and every step could be a new beginning or a final farewell.

This is a story of lost roots, hidden faces, and the courage it takes to walk a path not just to escape, but to create.

1: The Arrival

The Face I Saw Once, carries that haunting weight of memory, mystery, and the search for truth.

It holds the story's core: the fleeting glimpse that sparks a journey through labyrinths of shadow and light, identity and discovery.

The man she kept in her purse—the faded photograph, worn at the edges—was more than a picture. It was a silent thread pulling through time, linking the labyrinth's mysteries to her hidden past.

As you pieced it together, the truth crystallized: the man from London, the face marked WANTED, was the same man she had carried with her all along.

Her father.

Not a stranger, but a secret kept close, wrapped in shadow and silence.

The Spiral pulsed around you both, the walls whispering of lost connections and the fragile hope of reunion.

You met her eyes, voice steady but soft.

The man in your purse... he's the one you've been searching for.

Her breath caught—a moment suspended between fear and longing.

The labyrinth hadn't just led you through a maze of shadows. It had led you home.

Her fingers trembled as she held the photograph closer, tracing the lines of a face she'd only known in dreams and half-remembered stories.

The man's eyes seemed to hold a secret—a promise and a warning intertwined.

I never knew," she whispered, voice barely audible. "All this time... he was here, in the shadows.

The Spiral around you seemed to pulse stronger, as if the labyrinth itself recognized the moment—when lost pieces began to fit, and old wounds edged toward healing.

But the story wasn't finished.

The man's past, tangled in trade, shadows, and secrets darker than either of you could guess, was a path that stretched deeper into the maze.

The question hung in the air:

Would you follow the thread deeper—into the tunnels where truth and danger whispered side by side?

Or would you step back, holding the fragile hope of discovery close, and decide what to do with this newfound truth?

The Spiral waits, endless and alive—ready to turn again.

The air grew heavy with unspoken tension as you both stood at the labyrinth's edge—caught between the comfort of what you'd uncovered and the peril that lay ahead.

Her eyes met yours, fierce with determination yet shadowed by doubt.

We have to know, she said softly. If he's really my father... if there's more to his story. I need to understand.

You nodded, feeling the weight of choice settle deep in your bones.

Together, you stepped into the tunnel—where darkness swallowed the light but secrets waited patiently.

Every echo, every whisper, seemed to pulse with life, guiding you toward truths buried beneath years of silence and fear.

The Spiral wasn't just a maze anymore—it was a mirror, reflecting the complexity of human existence, the ties that bind, and the courage to face the unknown.

With each step, you moved closer to the man whose face had haunted shadows and memories alike.

And to the answer that could change everything.

The city breathed beneath a veil of mist as I stepped off the train in Prague, the chill in the air tugging at memories I didn't fully understand yet.

The café was the same—the smell of dark roast, the quiet clatter of cups, and the barista who recognized me with a knowing nod.

It was here, in this unassuming place, that I first saw her—the woman whose eyes held stories I was only beginning to unravel.

And somewhere, deep beneath the city's cobblestones, the Spiral pulsed—alive with secrets waiting to be uncovered.

I never imagined that a single glance, a face seen once, would lead me into a labyrinth of shadows, whispers, and a truth tangled with love, loss, and a man I thought I'd never find.

She pulled the worn photograph from her purse, the edges soft and faded like a memory slipping through time.

That man, she said, voice barely above a whisper, he's been with me longer than I can remember. My mother kept it hidden, never spoke his name.

I traced the lines of the face—sharp, tired, but unmistakably the man we'd seen in London, the one marked WANTED in the shadows of the labyrinth.

Do you think he's your father? I asked, the weight of the question pressing between us like the thick Prague fog.

She nodded slowly, eyes searching mine for answers she wasn't sure I had.

The Spiral brought me here," she said. "And now I think it's leading me to him.

The labyrinth was no longer just a puzzle. It was a path—a fragile thread connecting past secrets with a future we had yet to write.

The entrance to the tunnels yawned before us—dark, cold, and whispering with the weight of untold stories.

The faint glow of a single lantern cast long shadows, dancing on walls etched with symbols that seemed to pulse with the Spiral's rhythm.

With every step, the air grew thicker—laden with secrets buried deep beneath the city, where time folded in on itself and memories tangled with fear.

This is where he disappeared, she said, voice steady but eyes betraying a flicker of doubt. Where the man from the photograph vanished without a trace.

We pressed on, guided by fragments—a discarded watch, a torn piece of paper with a name barely legible, and the faintest echo of a whisper that felt like a warning.

The labyrinth was more than a place. It was a living thing, shifting with every choice we made, every fear we faced.

And somewhere in its depths, the truth waited—patient, hidden, and dangerous.

The tunnels gave way to a hidden chamber, dust thick in the air, and walls lined with fading canvases—unfinished stories frozen in time.

One painting caught your eye: a portrait of the man from the photograph, his gaze haunting and distant, painted with strokes that seemed almost alive.

A plaque beneath it bore the painter's name—someone whispered of only in fragments, a man who vanished as mysteriously as the subject he immortalized.

She must have known, your friend murmured, fingers brushing the cracked frame. The painter... he saw something. Something he couldn't forget.

Suddenly, the air shifted—the Spiral's pulse quickened, as if warning you that some truths demand sacrifice, and some stories refuse to stay buried.

The labyrinth's walls seemed to close in, urging you forward—or warning you to turn back.

The portrait's eyes followed you, a silent challenge.

The portrait's gaze lingered as if daring you to look closer—beyond the brushstrokes and into the hidden truth beneath.

Whispers from the labyrinth echoed in your mind: a trader, a man tangled in the shadows of a forgotten mafia, his past stained with secrets darker than the tunnels themselves.

He wasn't just a missing man, you whispered. He was hunted.

Your friend's breath caught. That's why my mother kept his photo hidden... she was protecting me—from who, I don't know yet.

The Spiral's pulse grew urgent, and you felt the weight of the labyrinth press against your skin—this was no longer just a search for a man, but a confrontation with a legacy of fear, power, and survival.

With every step, deeper, the line between hunter and hunted blurred.

And somewhere, in the shadows of the father's past, a final revelation awaited—one that could change everything.

Deeper into the labyrinth, the air grew thick with silence—broken only by the distant drip of water echoing like a heartbeat.

You found a worn leather journal tucked beneath loose stones, its pages yellowed but intact.

Inside, the man from the photograph wrote not just of deals and dangers, but of love lost and promises broken.

He had tried to protect his family from the shadows closing in—choices made in desperation, secrets buried to keep them safe.

A final entry stopped abruptly, a cryptic note: If you find this, know that I never stopped searching for the light beyond the Spiral.

Your friend's eyes filled with tears—a mixture of grief and hope.

The labyrinth was no longer just a maze of mystery; it was a testament to a father's fractured love and a daughter's relentless quest.

And somewhere, beyond the shadows and secrets, the path forward was waiting—for healing, for truth, and for the courage to face what comes next.

The tunnels opened into a cavern bathed in a faint, ethereal glow—stones carved with symbols of protection and passage.

Here, time felt suspended, as if the labyrinth itself held its breath.

Your friend stepped forward, clutching the journal, eyes shining with resolve.

This is where his story doesn't end, she said. Where I choose to write the next chapter.

A soft wind stirred, carrying with it a whisper—a promise that no matter how tangled the past, the future remains unwritten.

You both stood at the edge of the Spiral, ready to step beyond fear, beyond mystery.

Because sometimes, the greatest journey is not to find the face you once saw—

But to discover the face you want to become.

The labyrinth has led you here.

Now, the path is yours.

I saw the face once—only once.

On a rainy street in London.

In the reflection of a café window, where the world seemed paused for a heartbeat.

He didn't look at me. He looked past me.

Or maybe through me.

There was something fractured in his expression—like he knew he'd already disappeared.

I thought nothing of it until years later, when my friend pulled a photograph from her purse.

Faded. Torn.

The same man.

She said it had belonged to her mother, who had died with too many secrets.

She never knew her father.

Never even knew his name.

But that moment—that face was the thread that pulled us both into something far deeper.

A city of echoes.

A painter who vanished.
A labyrinth that lives.
And a truth that waited patiently in the dark.
That's how it begins.
Not with answers.
But with a glimpse.
Of a face, I saw once.

2: - The letter

The train slowed as it pulled into Prague. The sky was bruised with dusk, and the buildings leaned inward like old keepers of secrets. I stepped onto the platform, luggage in one hand, notebook in the other, and that familiar pull tightening in my chest.

I didn't come here looking for him. Not really.

But something had changed since London. Since that flash of a face photo from her mother's purse. The same eyes. The same scar. The same absence.

And now, here I was, following a shadow.

The café sat just beyond the square, quiet and warm, with the scent of strong coffee and old wood. The barista gave a nod, as if I'd never left. And in a way, I hadn't.

That table in the corner was where I first saw her.

She was there again.

Same coat. Same distant gaze. Same silence full of questions.

She didn't speak until I sat across from her.

I remembered something, she said, not looking at me. About the painting. The one I dreamed about as a child. I think it's real. And I think he's in it.

I didn't ask how she knew. I'd stopped questioning the Spiral's logic a long time ago.

We drank in silence, and the walls around us seemed to bend just slightly—like the city itself was listening.

Outside, the wind shifted.

And below our feet, the labyrinth stirred.

The hidden chamber breathed with dust and silence. The paintings leaned against the stone like they'd been waiting.

And there—at the center—hung the one that stopped everything.

Her hand flew to her mouth. That's him.

The man in the portrait.

The face from the photograph.

The father she never knew.

But it wasn't just his face. The painting... moved. Not physically—but emotionally. It shifted. His expression was sorrow and warning, a man burdened by what he couldn't say in life.

And at the bottom corner, almost hidden in the darkened brushwork: a signature. Not a name.

A symbol. The Spiral.

You both stared at it.

I remember this, she whispered. "Not from seeing it. From dreaming it.

And suddenly, it clicked—the painter wasn't just an artist. He was involved. He had seen something. Maybe he knew the father. Maybe he'd hidden something in the paint. Or behind it.

You stepped closer. The canvas trembled—just slightly.

A draft of air behind the frame. Hollow.

You exchanged a glance, then reached behind the painting. Your fingers found a small metal latch—nearly invisible.

Click.

The wall opened.

Darkness. Cold. A staircase descending into earth.

Paintings didn't just capture the past here.

They guarded the truth.

The staircase behind the painting spiraled downward—narrow, ancient, carved directly into stone. The air smelled of oil, dust, and something older, something forgotten.

You held the lantern high, shadows flickering against the walls. She followed close, clutching the journal you'd found earlier, pages still marked with her father's final entry.

At the bottom, the stairs opened into a vaulted chamber—low ceilings, walls lined with wooden crates and stacks of canvas under cloth.

In the center stood an easel. Empty.

But the floor beneath it was stained—not with paint. With something darker.

A dried pool. Long ago. Left behind.

This is where the painter disappeared, you murmured.

She nodded. And where my father may have come... for answers. Or for silence.

You began opening the crates. One by one, more unfinished paintings emerged—half-faces, twisted labyrinths, maps embedded in brushstrokes, symbols layered like code.

And then—at the bottom of a crate—you found it:

A sketchbook.

Inside: the same face. Over and over. Expressions changing. Ages shifting. Like the painter had been haunted by the man.

And one final sketch: the face, surrounded by shadows, a child in his arms.

Her hand trembled. That's me...

You both froze.

A sound.

A shuffle behind the wall.

Not memory this time.

Movement.

Someone was still down here.

And they didn't want the past uncovered.

The sound came again—closer now. A footstep, deliberate. Then a breath. Not yours.

You killed the lantern.

Darkness swallowed the room, but your ears sharpened. You felt her hand slip into yours, tight, like a tether to the only thing still certain.

A sliver of light broke through a seam in the far wall—then vanished.

Whoever it was, they knew these tunnels better than you did.

You whispered, we can't outrun what we don't understand.

She nodded, silent.

You opened the sketchbook again, flipping past the familiar face. At the very back, a page had been torn—but a fragment remained.

An address. Prague. Smudged, but legible.

And a name.

Not her father's.

The painter's.

E. Novak.

She inhaled sharply. My mother once mentioned that name.

You looked back toward the sound—gone now, but the pressure remained.

This was never just about your father, you whispered. It was about what he was trying to hide. And what someone else is trying to keep buried.

You grabbed the sketchbook, stuffed it into your coat, and moved toward the stair.

But as you reached the first step—something clicked behind you.

A recorder.

Tucked into the wall. Still running.

And before you could react, a voice hissed softly from a hidden speaker:

Stop digging.

Then silence.

Just the Spiral pulsing faintly beneath your feet.

Chapter Five: The Name in the Shadows

You didn't speak. Just climbed the steps fast, the sketchbook under your arm, her breath steady behind you.

Whoever left that warning—they were close, and they wanted you scared.

But fear now felt different. Sharper. Focused.

Back in the café's dim light, you laid out the journal and the sketchbook side by side. Clues. Fragments. Whispers left behind.

She traced the name again: E. Novak.

He wasn't just a painter, she murmured. He was... a witness. Maybe even a messenger.

You flipped the journal back to the entry with the Spiral—the father's last message.

If you find this, know I never stopped searching for the light beyond the Spiral.

What light?

A cipher appeared on the page—ink that hadn't been visible before, now surfacing under the café's golden bulb.

A sequence of symbols. Coordinates? Or a code?

Your phone buzzed.

No caller ID.

You picked it up. Silence.

Then: a voice you'd never heard, low and urgent.

E. Novak isn't dead. He's waiting.

Click.

The line went dead.

You looked at her. We go to the address.

She nodded. Let's finish what they tried to bury.

Outside, the street was quiet—but you both felt it.

The Spiral had widened.

And the next turn could change everything.

The address led you to the edge of Malá Strana, where the streets narrowed and history clung to the walls like damp moss. The building stood half-forgotten—three stories high, shutters closed, its paint weathered to silence.

Number 27

You approached slowly. No name on the buzzer. Just a single brass spiral carved into the doorframe—small, deliberate.

He marked it, she whispered.

You knocked. Nothing. Then pushed. It opened without resistance.

Inside, dust floated like memory. The scent of turpentine, old paper, and something fainter—cedar, still lingered.

Paintings lined the hallway, turned toward the wall. None bore signatures.

But there were symbols. Over and over.

In the center of the sitting room: a canvas draped in black cloth.

You hesitated.

Then pulled it back.

It wasn't a painting.

It was a mirror, framed by wood carved in spirals.

And in its reflection...

Not your faces.

But his.

The man from the photograph. Alive. Standing behind you.

You spun.

No one there.

She stepped closer. It's not just a mirror. It's... something else. A memory trap?

On the floor beneath it, a leather folder.

Inside: letters. Newspaper clippings. And one photograph.

The painter, Novak. Standing beside your friend's father.

Not young. Not old.

And dated two years ago.

They knew each other, you said.

And maybe, she added, voice trembling, they still do.

From deeper in the house, a creak.

Then: a voice.

Rough. A whisper pulled through years.

You shouldn't have come.

You didn't speak. Just exchanged a glance with her—a silent agreement.

Observe first. Then act.

You moved quietly, the floorboards soft beneath your feet, following the sound down a narrow hall. Dust motes danced in the light from a cracked window. At the end: a studio door, slightly ajar, humming with stillness.

Inside, the walls were covered in paintings—but not of people.

Maps. Spirals. Doors. Eyes.

Symbols hidden in brush strokes, cities twisted like mazes, faces half-formed in the paint.

And in the middle of the room, hunched over a table lit by a single lamp—a man.

Hair white, hands stained with pigment, a tremor in his posture that spoke of years hiding from the world.

You stepped closer.

He didn't flinch.

You're looking for the wrong man, he rasped without turning. But the right truth.

She moved beside you. Are you Novak?

He nodded slowly.

Then turned—eyes sunken but clear. A knowing look.

You carry her eyes, he said to her. Like she did.

My mother? she asked.

No, Novak whispered. The other one. The one he lost. The one we all lost.

He gestured toward a canvas—still wet.

It showed the man from the photograph again. But this time, he was walking into the Spiral. Not away.

Your father, Novak said, was not just running. He was guarding something. From people who never stopped hunting it.

He pulled out a single envelope. Sealed with wax.

Her name on the front.

This is his last message, he said. But once you open it, there's no turning back.

She held it, frozen.

Then looked at you. We open it.

Novak nodded. Then I hope you're ready.

The Spiral never offers answers without a cost.

Her fingers hovered over the wax seal. A deep red spiral stamped into it—elegant, intentional. Something ancient. Something final.

You watched her breathe once, then break it.

Inside: one page. A letter, handwritten in ink that had bled slightly with time. The edges curled, as if it had waited too long to be read.

She unfolded it.

And read aloud:

My daughter,

If this has found you, then the spiral has turned once more. I could never tell you the truth when it would've broken you... but the world you live in is not the one you were born into.

You are not just my child.

You are the keeper of a door I once opened and could never close.

The Spiral is alive. It remembers. And it chose you.

There are those who will follow the trail—people who believe what I found must be buried forever. But if you choose to walk forward... don't walk alone.

Find the mirror that reflects no face.

Find the door that opens to no room.

And when you stand in the center of the Spiral, speak the word only your mother ever whispered.

Then you'll know who you really are.

Then you'll know who you really are.

I loved you more than I feared what you'd become.

Your Father.

Her fingers hovered over the wax seal. A deep red spiral stamped into it—elegant, intentional. Something ancient. Something final.

You watched her breathe once, then break it.

The room seemed too still. Even Novak looked away.

She never whispered anything to me, she said softly.

Not to you, Novak replied. But maybe to herself. The Spiral remembers everything. Even words left unspoken.

You turned toward the paintings again.

There, in the corner of one—so faint you might have missed it—was a title:

The Mirror with No Face.

You stepped closer.

And behind the canvas, etched in the wood:

Coordinates.

The next location.

The Spiral had opened the path again.

Shadows of the Past.

You decide to press Novak for the truth, there was more, and you both knew it.

He sighed, rubbing his temples, as if the weight of years pressed down on him.

The Spiral isn't just a symbol, he began. It's a curse—and a promise. Your father stumbled onto something that threatened powerful people.

Smugglers, traders... shadows who use Prague's underground like a chessboard.

He paused.

I was the painter who tried to capture it all—the secret routes, the faces, the deals made in darkness. But I vanished because I refused to stay silent. I paid the price. Your father? He tried to protect you by keeping his distance.

She swallowed hard. So, the man in the photo—my father—he wasn't running because he was afraid of me. He was running for me.

Novak nodded slowly. Yes. But running only delays what must be faced.

He handed you a folded map, worn and marked with spirals and cryptic symbols.

This leads to the Mirror with No Face. That's where the Spiral reveals its deepest secret.

Outside, the wind whispered through the old city.

The Spiral was calling you forward.

And whatever waited at the Mirror... would change everything.

The Mirror with No Face

The map guided you through Prague's twisting streets until you reached an old, forgotten chapel beneath the city—a place where shadows gathered like mist.

The entrance was hidden beneath cracked cobblestones, a narrow stairway spiraling down into damp silence.

You descended, hearts pounding with a mixture of fear and purpose.

At the bottom, a chamber opened—walls lined with cracked mirrors, some shattered, some fogged over with time.

At the center stood a single mirror—tall, ornate, but its surface was dark, like polished obsidian.

You stepped forward.

Her voice broke the silence: The Mirror with No Face.

You looked into it together.

At first, nothing.

Then slowly, the dark surface shimmered—images flickering like distant memories.

Faces appeared—hers, yours, her father's—and then one by one, they blurred, fading into a spiral of shadows.

And in the center, a word emerged.

Remember.

A whisper filled the room—soft, urgent.

You are not who you think you are, it said.

You are the key.

The Spiral had brought you here for a reason.

To unlock the door your father never could.

Her lips parted, trembling.

I remember now, she whispered. A word... just once, when I was a child. Vratit— to return.(Vratit cu, I will return)

You nodded. Then say it.

Together, you spoke the word into the darkness.

The mirror pulsed, the obsidian surface rippling like water.

A hidden door slid open behind it, revealing a narrow passage glowing faintly with golden light.

Beyond lay the heart of the Spiral — a place where past and future blurred, where truth waited naked and raw.

As you stepped inside, the weight of all that had been hidden pressed around you.

But with each step, you felt lighter.

Because here, in the labyrinth's core, the story was no longer about running or hiding.

It was about becoming.

The Spiral was no longer a trap.

It was a beginning.

The passage led you into a vast chamber bathed in soft, golden light that seemed to pulse with the rhythm of your own heartbeat.

Walls carved with spirals and cryptic symbols glowed faintly, as if alive.

In the center, a pedestal held a small, ancient box—ornate, locked, but warm to the touch.

She reached for it, hesitating. This... this must be what my father protected.

You nodded. Whatever's inside could change everything.

The lock clicked open without resistance.

Inside, you found a folded parchment and a simple key.

The parchment was a map—not of places, but of moments. Moments where the Spiral bent time and memory.

A final note, written in the same familiar hand:

To break the cycle, you must choose:

Walk the Spiral alone and find your own path,

Or walk with others and rewrite its meaning.

She looked at you, eyes shining with tears and resolve.

This is our choice.

The labyrinth was no longer just a puzzle.

It was a story you could change.

Together.

She squeezed your hand, steadying the storm inside both of you.

We don't have to do this alone, she said softly. The Spiral shaped our lives, but maybe we can shape its end.

You nodded. Then we find who else this touches—the lost, the seekers. Together, we'll rewrite the story.

Outside, the chamber's golden light dimmed, folding back into shadow. The labyrinth was waiting, but now it hummed with possibility.

The spiral was no longer a curse — it was a legacy.

A map to who you were, who you could be.

And as you stepped back into the twisting tunnels of Prague, the unknown no longer whispered fear.

It sang a promise.

The face you saw once was only the beginning.

The true journey was just unfolding.

As you and she emerged from the chamber, the labyrinth seemed to breathe with you—its walls no longer cold and confining, but alive and watching.

The streets of Prague outside felt different, too—full of hidden pathways, unspoken stories waiting to be told.

Together, you vowed to find the others—the scattered pieces of this spiral-shaped puzzle.

To unearth secrets buried in shadows, to confront the ghosts that haunted your pasts.

And maybe, just maybe, to build a new future from the fragments of the unknown.

Because sometimes, the face you saw once is a key, not a conclusion.

And every labyrinth, no matter how twisted, leads somewhere.

Let's introduce her—the first of the others.

Her name is Lena, a cryptic archivist with a sharp mind and a guarded past. She holds pieces of the Spiral's story hidden in forgotten manuscripts and whispered legends.

You find her in a dusty library deep in the city, surrounded by stacks of old books.

Lena looks up, eyes curious but cautious.

You're not the first to seek the Spiral's truth, she says, voice low. And I doubt you'll be the last.

She holds out a worn journal. This belonged to my grandfather. He chased the same shadows. Maybe together, we can finally end the spiral's cycle.

3: The Archivist's Secret

Lena's fingers brushed over the leather-bound journal as if it were a fragile relic, its pages worn but alive with secrets.

I've pieced together fragments, she said, from Prague's underground to forgotten family letters. The Spiral isn't just a symbol—it's a living thread weaving through generations.

She flipped open the journal, revealing sketches—maps of tunnels beneath the city, hidden rooms, and coded letters.

Here, she pointed to a faded note, my grandfather mentioned a gathering. A meeting of those who knew the Spiral's power, and feared it. They called themselves The Keepers.

You leaned closer. The words felt like a key turning in a lock.

They believed the Spiral could reshape fate, Lena continued, but it needed a guardian. Someone who could walk its depths without losing themselves.

She looked at you both.

Maybe that's why your father disappeared. Maybe that's why the Spiral called you.

The labyrinth was growing.

And with Lena, the path forward was clearer—and more dangerous.

The Keepers

The name echoed in your mind—The Keepers, a secret society intertwined with the labyrinth's shadows, guardians of a power no one dared control.

Lena traced a route on the journal's map, leading beneath the city to an abandoned crypt below the Church of St. Nicholas.

Here, she said, they met. Sworn to protect the Spiral's secret—or to bury it forever.

The air grew colder as you descended through narrow tunnels carved from stone.

Faint symbols glowed on the walls—spirals, eyes, and words in an ancient script neither of you recognized.

Ahead, a heavy iron door stood ajar.

Inside, relics lay scattered—candles half-melted, papers with cryptic codes, and a broken mirror, its surface cracked but still shimmering.

Suddenly, a shadow moved.

A voice whispered from the darkness.

You've come far. But the Spiral demands a price.

You step forward cautiously, eyes adjusting to the dim light.

I'm not here to fight, you say. We seek answers. About the Spiral. About the man in the photo. About what we're meant to do.

The shadow shifts—then steps into the flickering candlelight.

An older woman, her gaze sharp and knowing.

I am Marika, she says softly. One of the last Keepers.

She holds up a faded medallion etched with the Spiral symbol.

Your father was part of us once. He tried to protect you by stepping away.

She studies your friend closely. But the Spiral never forgets blood. And now it calls you both.

Marika's voice lowers.

There is a ritual—one that can break the cycle or bind it forever.

She offers a choice: face the ritual now, risking all you know, or gather more knowledge to prepare.

You exchange a look with her—a silent pact sealed in determination.

We face it now, she says, voice steady.

Marika nods, lighting a circle of candles around the cracked mirror.

The Spiral's power is ancient, she explains. This ritual will test your bond, your memories, your fears. Only those who confront the darkness within can reshape what lies beyond.

She hands you both small tokens—charms carved from bone and glass.

Hold these. They will anchor you when the Spiral twists reality.

The chamber grows colder. The mirror begins to ripple, swallowing the candlelight.

You step inside the circle together, hearts pounding.

The Spiral awakens.

A flicker—a fragment of a memory, hazy but vivid.

You see a young boy in a dimly lit room, clutching the same spiral medallion Marika holds now.

He's frightened, hiding from shadows that whisper secrets too heavy for his age.

Then the scene shifts.

A woman's voice—soft, urgent—echoes in the dark:

Remember who you are. The Spiral chooses its keepers.

Suddenly, you're pulled back, heart racing.

The room blurs, the mirror's surface trembling.

Beside you, she gasps—her eyes wide with recognition.

This... this is my father.

The Spiral's grip tightens.

The ritual has begun.

You take a deep breath, feeling the weight of the memory settle like a puzzle piece snapping into place.

This isn't just a glimpse, you say, voice steady. It's a direction. A key.

She nods, eyes still shining with recognition. He was trying to protect me... to send a message.

Marika steps closer, her voice grave. The Spiral's power feeds on forgotten truths. You must follow these memories—they are the thread through the labyrinth.

The tokens in your hands pulse softly, anchoring you both to reality as the visions deepen.

The chamber fades, replaced by a swirling map of light and shadow—paths converging on a single point deep beneath Prague.

The next step is clear:

Find the hidden vault beneath the old city archives—where the final secret waits.

The Spiral is guiding you closer to Archives.

The city's pulse quickened as you made your way to the old archives—a grand, forgotten building rumored to house secrets no map dared reveal.

Lena's journal guided you through hidden passages, cobwebbed stairwells, and locked doors long untouched.

Finally, beneath a loose floor tile, you found a narrow iron ladder descending into cold darkness.

The air smelled of earth and history.

You climbed down, tokens glowing faintly, casting eerie shadows on stone walls covered in cryptic markings.

At the end of the tunnel, a heavy door stood, bearing the Spiral symbol carved deep into its surface.

You pressed the tokens against the door.

With a grinding sound, it slowly creaked open, revealing a chamber filled with relics—a dusty desk, old letters, and a large canvas covered in a faded cloth.

As you pulled the cloth away, the painting beneath revealed itself—a portrait of the man from London, but older, wearied, eyes haunted yet resolute.

Underneath, a folded letter was pinned.

Your hands trembled as you read the first lines:

If you've found this, the Spiral has chosen you. My daughter, my blood — you must understand. The path ahead is treacherous, but in truth lies freedom.

The labyrinth's final secret waits.

You look at her. Her hands hover above the letter, hesitant—then steady.

Read it, you whisper.

She unfolds it carefully. The ink is faded but still legible, each word written with urgency, as if her father knew time was running out.

My name is Elias Vora. If you are reading this, then the Spiral has brought you to where I failed to go. I was one of The Keepers—but I broke our vow. I fell in love, and from that love, you were born.

They said the Spiral would demand a price. I thought I could pay it alone, keep you safe by vanishing. But the Spiral doesn't forget. Nor does it forgive.

There's a vault beneath this chamber. It holds the true map—not the one of tunnels or cities, but of lives. Names. The bloodline the Spiral has followed for centuries. Yours is the final name.

Her hands tremble.

You must choose: burn the vault and end the Spiral's hold over us all... or open it, and claim what waits inside. Knowledge. Power. But with it, the burden I could never bear.

She lowers the letter, silent.

Beneath your feet, a faint click, a hidden panel begins to shift.

Stone slides. A staircase reveals itself, descending into darkness below the chamber.

The Spiral holds its breath.

Without a word, she steps forward.

The letter still in hand, her eyes fixed on the dark stairwell.

You follow her, the echo of your footsteps blending with the low hum of something ancient stirring beneath the earth.

The stairs spiral downward—carved from black stone, slick with time. The air is heavy, charged, as if the past is watching.

At the bottom: a circular chamber bathed in cold blue light.

In the center stands the Vault, a smooth, obsidian structure with no visible keyhole or handle. Just the Spiral etched deep into its surface.

As she approaches, the medallion around her neck begins to glow faintly.

The Spiral responds.

A low rumble sounds, and the vault opens silently, revealing what lies within:

Scrolls bound in blood-red thread.

Photographs of faces across decades.

And a single mirror—tall, cracked, but glowing from within.

Etched into its base:

The Spiral ends where truth is seen.

She turns to you.

This... this is the story behind everything. My father. The Keepers. Us.

You nod, stepping toward the mirror.

Your reflection shimmers—then begins to change. Not your face... but his,

Elias. Watching you. Waiting.

A voice, faint but clear:

You hold the final thread. Will you sever it—or weave it into something new?

The Spiral is no longer a myth.

It's a choice.

She steps beside you, her gaze locked on the mirror—on the reflection of the man she's never truly known, yet carries in every breath.

I see him, she whispers. But I also see me. Not as a child of shadows... but as someone who can choose.

The Spiral pulses once—soft, like a heartbeat.

Then again—louder, deeper.

The vault begins to shift around you, the scrolls unrolling on their own, revealing names, moments, memories not lived but inherited.

You step forward.

And the mirror speaks—not with words, but sensation: every forgotten choice, every silenced truth, every path you might have walked.

You are being asked to decide:

Sever the Spiral, burn the scrolls, seal the chamber, and end the ancient thread of power and memory once and for all.

Or—

Weave it anew, take the knowledge, reshape the labyrinth, and become not just walkers of the Spiral, but its new keepers.

She looks at you, tears in her eyes—but they are not of fear. They are of clarity.

What we do now... becomes the story they'll find next.

So:

Do you burn the Spiral and walk away free?

Or do you take its threads—and begin to rewrite the Spiral itself?

You meet her gaze.

No more running. No more fear.

We rewrite it, you say.

She nods, and together, you step toward the vault. The scrolls pulse softly—threads of lives long gone waiting to be woven into something new.

She takes one, gently unrolling it. Her father's name. Her mother's. Then hers.

With a slow, steady breath, she adds the first new name: hers and yours, together.

The mirror flickers—then begins to glow with warm light. Not cold prophecy. But possibility.

The Spiral no longer twists in endless repetition.

It expands—open-ended, alive.

A quiet shift passes through the chamber, as if history itself exhales.

And above, far above, in the city that doesn't know what just happened beneath its feet, the bells of Prague begin to ring.

Not as a warning.

But as a beginning.

The city slept beneath a restless sky, its streets slick with rain and secrets. But for you, sleep was a stranger now.

The Spiral you once rewrote had shifted—and with it, something deeper stirred in the shadows. The woman by your side held the key, but even she didn't yet know what doors it might unlock.

A whisper led you both to the edge of the labyrinth again—not the one beneath Prague, but a new maze hidden in plain sight. Its corridors twisted through forgotten ruins, tangled forests, and memories half-buried in time.

There, a new thread unraveled: a map etched not in stone, but in reflections—fragments of faces and stories you hadn't yet seen. The mirror had shown you a future, but now it was calling you to chase what had been left behind.

As you step into the unknown, you feel it—the pulse of the Spiral, beating faster, pulling you deeper.

The adventure begins. The mystery unfolds.

And the labyrinth waits.

You glance at her—eyes reflecting the faint glow of a weathered compass in her hand. The needle spins wildly, refusing to settle.

It's not just any map, she says quietly. It's alive. Like the Spiral... but unpredictable.

A sudden crack in the sky splits the silence, and rain begins to fall heavier. Each drop feels like a call, urging you forward.

Together, you push through the tangle of undergrowth, the labyrinth's edges blurring between reality and something else—something older.

The trees seem to whisper, shadows folding into themselves, revealing paths where none should be.

Ahead, a shattered statue—its face worn away, but the Spiral still faintly visible at its base.

She kneels, tracing the symbol with trembling fingers.

This is where it begins, she breathes.

You step closer, heart pounding.

The labyrinth is no longer just a place. It's a living puzzle, and you hold the first piece.

One wrong move could trap you forever.

But turning back is no longer an option.

As the rain thickened, the air grew heavy with a scent both familiar and strange—earth mixed with something metallic, like rust or old blood.

The broken statue seemed to pulse beneath her touch, the Spiral glowing faintly, casting eerie shadows on the damp ground.

Suddenly, the compass's needle snapped to a steady point, directing toward a narrow passage hidden behind a curtain of hanging vines.

You exchanged a look, the unspoken question hanging between you: Are we ready to step deeper?

With a steadying breath, you moved forward, pushing aside the curtain.

The passage narrowed, walls closing in like the pages of a forgotten book.

Whispers floated just beyond hearing—fragments of a language lost to time.

Your footsteps echoed, swallowed quickly by the dark.

Then, just ahead, a faint light flickered.

Not from torches. Something else.

A glow emanating from the walls themselves—symbols emerging, shifting, alive.

The labyrinth was waking.

And it was watching.

Your adventure had become a test—not only of courage, but of what you were willing to uncover... and what you might have to leave behind.

The glow intensified—not blinding, but steady—revealing walls carved with scenes you didn't remember living, yet felt carved into your bones. A child standing at a train station. A woman hiding a letter inside a hollow book. A man's silhouette turning away just before a face could be seen.

Her breath caught. These are... memories. Not mine. Not yours. Inherited.

The Spiral wasn't just a path—it was a vessel. A container for untold histories, carried forward through blood and silence.

She reached out toward one carving—a cracked window with a man's blurred reflection. The wall gave way.

A chamber opened.

Inside: mirrors. Dozens of them, mismatched, weathered, hung at every angle. But none reflected you.

Only the man from the portrait. The one she carried in her purse.

In each mirror, a different moment of his life—him walking through London, sitting in a café, exchanging an envelope with someone whose face remained forever turned.

And then in one—he saw you.

You stepped back.

He knew, you whispered.

The Spiral had not just led you to him.

He had left it for you.

She stared at the mirror where the man—her father—locked eyes with your reflection, as if time had folded in on itself.

No, she whispered. This isn't just memory. This is navigation.

Each mirror, a door. Each scene, a key.

You stepped closer, the mirror's surface trembling like water held in stillness too long. The man inside raised his hand—not a wave, but a gesture. Three fingers. Then two. Then one.

The mirror blinked black.

Silence.

Then a faint click, echoed through the chamber. One of the mirrors—a small, cracked one on the far end—swung open like a door.

Behind it: darkness. Cold. Breathing.

You lit your small torch and stepped through first.

A long corridor stretched before you, lined with paintings. But they weren't complete—unfinished figures, half-seen eyes, hands suspended mid-motion. Like someone had started telling stories but was pulled away just before the truth was revealed.

She followed, slowly. Her voice barely above a breath: "He wasn't just hiding. He was building something. Leaving a trail."

Then you both saw it—at the end of the corridor, a canvas turned to the wall. Untouched. Waiting.

And beside it: the same Spiral etched in blood-red.

Your name was written beneath. Not hers.

This time... the labyrinth wasn't just leading you.

It was calling you out.

She turned to you, pale but steady. "Why your name?"

You didn't answer. Not because you didn't want to—but because you couldn't. A weight settled in your chest, something you hadn't felt before: recognition without memory.

The canvas seemed to breathe. As you approached, fine dust lifted from its surface. A faint warmth pulsed beneath the fibers, as if something inside had been waiting for your touch.

You reached out.

The moment your fingers grazed the edge, the entire corridor flickered. A low hum rose—deep and ancient—like the groan of something buried shifting in its sleep.

The canvas turned itself.

On it: a half-formed portrait. A man—older now—but undeniably you. Standing beside him, a shadowed figure, her features obscured but unmistakable in presence.

She painted this, your companion murmured. Whoever the original painter was... it wasn't just a memory. It was a prophecy.

The Spiral beneath your name began to turn.

And then, without warning, the walls cracked open, revealing a circular chamber of stone. At its center: a pedestal.

Resting atop it...

A second photograph.

Of the man.

The woman.

And you.

As a child.

But none of you had ever taken that photo.

Had you?

The photograph was aged—edges curled, colors fading into sepia—but the figures were clear. The man, his hand on the woman's shoulder. And between them, a child no older than five... your face unmistakable, though you had no memory of it being taken.

Your companion stared, breath caught. That's impossible.

You picked up the photo. The back was blank—except for a single word, handwritten in a precise, elegant script:

Return.

The Spiral on the floor beneath the pedestal flared with dull red light, and you heard it again—the hum, deeper now, like a pulse from underground.

She turned toward you. What if we haven't been uncovering the past—what if we've been circling the edge of something meant to pull us back in?

You looked down at the child in the photo.

You were the thread. Not just the seeker—but the origin.

The labyrinth wasn't made to trap you.

It was made from you.

A doorway opened behind the pedestal—rough stone steps leading downward, lit by the same shifting glow.

There was only one way forward now.

Through the Spiral.

Through memory.

Through time.

And into the truth none of you were ready for.

The steps spiraled down—tight, uneven, carved by hands that knew this path was never meant to be straight. With each step, the air grew colder, denser, as if memory itself pressed against your skin.

The photo burned faintly in your pocket. Not fire—but heat. Like it was alive. Or guiding.

She followed silently, her fingers grazing the damp wall, eyes darting toward shapes only she could see.

At the bottom: a chamber. Perfectly round. Stone walls smooth and seamless. No torches, no lights—yet everything glowed faintly, as if lit from within.

In the center stood an archway. Freestanding. Empty.

But when you stepped closer, the arch filled with moving images, like reflections in shifting water.

You saw the man again. Younger. Painting. Watching the door. Then older, holding the same photo you carried now. Then gone. Erased mid-frame.

The Spiral appeared again, this time etched above the arch.

And then—your voice. Echoing from inside the portal:

You've been here before.

You froze. So did she.

But the image didn't wait. It showed her mother, placing something inside a wall—the photo. A key. A page torn from a journal.

Then it turned black.

She clutched your arm, shaken. This isn't memory. It's a recording. No— a return path. Left for us.

You understood.

This wasn't the end of the labyrinth.

It was the entrance.

You stood before the archway, the realization sinking like weight into your spine:

Everything until now was the perimeter. The Spiral was never the trap. It was the keyhole.

The real door had just opened.

The moment your foot crossed the threshold, the chamber behind you vanished. No sound. No flash. Just gone.

The world warped.

You were now in a wide corridor—walls lined with frames, each holding a different version of a moment you thought you understood:

-A train leaving the station without you.

The woman holding the photo, but her eyes filled with tears you'd never seen.

Yourself, walking away from something—someone—but your face never turned.

She moved beside you, breath held, as if one wrong sound might shatter the illusion.

Then one frame caught her. She froze.

It was her mother. In a dim room, talking to the man—your man. The father.

Not hiding. Not running. Planning.

There were blueprints. A list of names. Dates. Places crossed out in red.

They were building something, she whispered passage. A message.

You reached for the edge of the frame, and your finger passed through

Another door.

On the other side: a spiral staircase, this one made of glass. Beneath it—layers of light and shadow, as if memories and time were stacked like strata.

We're not going deeper, you said, heart racing.

We're going back.

And somewhere at the core of it all...

He was waiting.

The man.

The painter.

The father.

The architect of the Spiral.

And the one secret left unspoken.

Your hand gripped the glass rail as the staircase spiraled downward—not into darkness, but into layers of time, suspended like thin veils. Each step carried a hum beneath your feet, like walking on memory itself.

The light changed with every level—cool blues, dusky golds, the dim flicker of candlelight, the sharp white of hospital corridors. Moments echoed here. Not sounds. Impressions.

She walked silently beside you, eyes drawn to the shifting air around the stairs. Occasionally, she reached out, brushing against something invisible—only for a brief flicker of a face, a word, a touch to appear and vanish again.

Then—you stopped.

A floor with no doors. Only a single easel at its center.

A painting. Covered in a cloth.

She approached it, heart in her throat. The silence was unbearable.

Then she pulled the cloth away.

It was him.

The man.

Her father.

But not painted from life. He was looking directly at the viewer, eyes full of something between regret and warning. In his hand: a pocket watch, open. Inside it, not time—but a photo of her as a baby.

And at the bottom of the canvas, scrawled hastily, in paint that looked like it had bled out of him.

Don't follow me further. Unless you're ready to lose everything, you thought was true.

The Spiral reappeared—this time behind the painting, embedded in the glass floor.

And it was turning.

Fast. Urgently.

As if trying to pull you down to the very origin of it all.

She looked at you. No fear now.

Just fire.

Let's finish what they started.

And with that, the floor gave way.

You both fell—into memory, into truth, into the burning heart of the labyrinth's final secret.

You didn't hit the ground.

You landed in a moment.

A room. Familiar but distorted—like a dream you couldn't name, yet knew was real.

The air was thick with oil paint, dust, and time. Faded newspapers scattered across a desk. A ticking sound—the pocket watch. And in the corner, half-shadowed by a curtain of pale light...

The man.

Older. Tired. Alive.

He didn't look up at first. He was painting. Furiously. Desperately. As if racing to finish before the memory itself collapsed.

You stepped forward, and the floor creaked.

He paused. Set the brush down.

Turned.

His eyes locked onto hers first.

Everything stopped.

My god...he whispered. You look like her.

She didn't speak. Couldn't. Her throat closed under the weight of years she hadn't lived but carried.

Then he looked at you. And smiled. Not with joy—but recognition.

You found it, he said quietly. The Spiral.

You nodded. You left it for us.

I had to, he said, voice cracking. They were closing in. The trail had to vanish behind me... until you were ready.

She stepped forward. Why did you disappear? Why the paintings, the mirrors, the doors?

He looked at the unfinished canvas beside him—one of a woman holding a child. Unnamed. Ageless.

Because truth isn't found in a single moment, he said. It's hidden between them. In fragments. The Spiral isn't a maze. It's a map. Of what was stolen. Of what you are.

You both stared, breathless.

Then he said, but you haven't come for answers, have you?

Silence.

You've come for the last piece.

He reached into his coat.

Pulled out a journal. Bound in cracked leather, held closed by a black thread.

This, he said, placing it in her hands, is her story. Your mother's. The parts she never told anyone. Not even me.

The Spiral shimmered behind you—dim now. Waiting.

One last decision.

Step back into the world with the truth...

Or stay, and finish the story from within.

The final thread had been placed in your hands.

And the labyrinth was listening.

She held the journal as if it might vanish. As if it had weight beyond pages—like memory, grief, and a thousand unsaid things had been stitched into its spine.

The man—her father—watched her with eyes worn from waiting. Not pleading. Just... hoping.

You glanced at the Spiral, its glow now pulsing slower, steadier. No longer pulling. Inviting.

She opened the journal.

The first page was blank. Then, faintly, ink began to bleed upward—as if summoned by touch. A name appeared. Hers.

Then her mother's handwriting, delicate but certain:

If you're reading this, the past has found you.

She read in silence. You watched her eyes shift—shock, then stillness. Her breath caught.

She looked up.

She knew, she said. All of it. The Spiral. The men who hunted him. Even me. She was part of something—not just running, but protecting.

The man nodded slowly. She was the beginning. I was the vessel. You...

He didn't finish.

She closed the journal softly. Her voice shook, but her spine didn't.

I'm not here to be protected anymore, she said. I'm here to remember. All of it.

The Spiral began to rise—lifting off the floor, forming a ring of light around the room. Pages from scattered books fluttered upward. Canvases shimmered. The air pulsed.

It was no longer a passage.

It was an awakening.

Then step through, her father said. Not as my daughter. Not as a seeker. But as the one who holds the story now.

She reached for your hand.

Together, you stepped into the light.

And as the Spiral closed behind you, a voice—hers, from the journal—whispered one final line:

The truth was never buried.

It was painted.
Layer by layer,
Waiting for you to see..........

4. Lost Inheritance, Spiral never truly ends.

The world you stepped into was not the world you left.

You walked together, hand in hand, the journal pressed between you like a compass. Her eyes weren't looking for signs anymore. They were reading the code, beneath them.

You stopped in front of a worn door in the old quarter of the city—one neither of you had ever noticed before. A faded mark carved into the wood. The same mark that had been in the photo. On the back of the canvas. In the ink of her mother's letter.

The Spiral was no longer hidden.

Inside: a room of clocks. Dozens of them. All ticking out of sync.

An old woman waited by the window, her hands folded over a walking stick carved with familiar patterns.

She didn't look surprised to see you.

I told your mother it would take three lifetimes for this to surface, she said, without turning. She was always so impatient.

The woman looked at your companion. Her gaze was sharp. Kind. And not of this time.

She left you the journal. But she didn't leave you the key.

The air shifted.

Then the woman pointed her cane toward the only clock not ticking.

Open it.

Inside, buried behind the gears: a slip of paper. A number. A name. And a location.

And a single sentence written in the same delicate handwriting: Your inheritance is not blood.

It is memory passed in silence.

The trail wasn't over.

It was beginning again.

But this time, you weren't lost.

This time, you were leading the Spiral.

The room seemed to pulse with the ticking of countless clocks, each one marking a fragmented heartbeat of the time itself. You held the slip of paper tightly, feeling the weight of the message as if it burned through the thin paper.

The name on the slip was unfamiliar. The number—an address deep in the city's oldest district. You glanced at her. Her eyes, once searching, now held quiet determination.

We have to go, she said, voice steady, almost like a command.

The old woman nodded slowly. Time does not heal. It conceals. And sometimes, it punishes. But it always leaves a thread.

The Spiral had woven itself into every corner of your lives. The labyrinth was no longer a place—it was the very fabric of your existence, stretching backward and forward, blurring past and future.

As you stepped out into the fading light of the city, the journal tucked safely in her bag, you realized this was more than a search for a man, a secret, or a truth.

This was a journey to reclaim a lost inheritance, one written in shadows, hidden in memories, and painted across the very paths you walked.

And the Spiral was guiding you—unraveling, twisting, pulling you deeper, into the mystery waiting just beyond the next turn.

You navigated the narrow, cobblestone streets as dusk settled, the city folding into shadows that seemed to breathe with ancient secrets. The address led you to a weathered building—its façade cracked, windows darkened by years of neglect.

The door creaked open before you even touched it.

Inside, the air was thick with the scent of old paper and wood smoke. Shelves lined with dusty tomes and faded photographs filled the dimly lit room. At the center, a desk bore a single envelope, yellowed with age.

She reached out, hesitating for a heartbeat, then opened it.

Inside, a letter, written in the same delicate script:

To the ones who walk the Spiral,

The path you follow is not just mine, but ours.

Each step uncovers what was hidden not only from the world but from ourselves.

Trust in the fragments—they hold the whole.

And when the final door opens, you will understand why the Spiral never truly ends.

Beneath the letter, a small key rested—ancient, ornate, and cold.

You looked at her.

She looked back.

This is the next step, she said softly. The Spiral isn't just around us. And now, it's time to unlock what's been waiting all along.

And the story had only just begun.

The key felt heavier than its size, as if burdened with years of secrets and silent promises. She turned it slowly between her fingers, eyes tracing every curve, every worn edge.

A sudden breeze swept through the room, though no windows were open. The shadows flickered.

You both knew—the door this key unlocked wasn't just physical. It was something deeper.

Together, you moved toward a corner where the wall seemed thicker, older. There—a faint outline of a doorframe, almost invisible beneath layers of plaster.

She inserted the key. It fit perfectly.

With a soft click, the wall shifted, revealing a narrow passage spiraling downward into darkness.

The Spiral's heartbeat thrummed stronger now, guiding you.

Ready? she whispered.

You nodded.

Stepping through, the world around you dissolved.

The labyrinth was no longer just a maze of stone and light—it was a journey through time, memory, and the soul.

Each step echoed with whispers of the past, promises of the future, and the fragile thread of now.

And somewhere deep inside, you knew—

This was where the true story waited to be told.

The air grew cooler as you descended, the narrow passage curling like a serpent swallowing you whole. The walls were rough, damp, and etched with symbols that seemed to shift when you blinked—spirals, eyes, fragmented faces.

Each step reverberated with the pulse of something ancient and alive.

She squeezed your hand. This place... it's where the Spiral begins.

Ahead, a faint glow appeared—a soft, flickering light casting long shadows that danced like ghosts.

At the end of the corridor, a heavy door stood ajar, revealing a chamber lined with mirrors.

But these were no ordinary mirrors. They reflected not your faces, but memories—fragments of moments lost, choices never made, secrets buried deep.

One mirror caught your eye. It showed the man from London, standing alone, looking over a cityscape cloaked in mist.

She whispered, He wasn't just a trader. He was a guardian of something... something that could unravel everything.

You stepped closer.

The mirror rippled.

And suddenly, you were no longer in the chamber.

You were standing beside him.

The Spiral had pulled you in—deeper into the story, deeper into the mystery that bound you all.

The journey wasn't over.

It had just begun.

You reached out instinctively, your hand passing through the glass surface like water, cool and real. The cityscape before you were no longer a reflection but a portal—a living moment frozen in time.

Beside the man from London, you felt the weight of history pressing down, thick with danger and whispered secrets. He glanced at you, eyes sharp but weary, as if sensing your presence though you were invisible to everyone else.

She's coming, he muttered, voice barely a breath. They always come when the Spiral moves.

Suddenly, shadows shifted behind the buildings—figures cloaked in darkness, their intentions clear and deadly.

Your heart raced.

The labyrinth was no longer just a map of memories. It was a battlefield.

And the man wasn't just a ghost from the past.

He was a warning.

You had to act—fast.

Who are they?" you whispered to her.

She tightened her grip on the journal.

Those who want to bury the Spiral forever. To erase the truth hidden in its twists.

The city faded around you, the mirror's surface rippling again.

You had a choice:

Step back into the chamber, armed with new knowledge, and prepare to face what was hunting you—

Or dive deeper, walk alongside the man from London, and uncover the secret that could change everything.

The Spiral was calling.

And this time, the stakes were higher than ever.

Without hesitation, you stepped forward, crossing the threshold into the scene unfolding before you. The cold air of the city night wrapped around you, blending with the tension hanging in the streets.

The man turned fully, locking eyes with you for a brief moment—a silent plea, or perhaps a test.

They call themselves The Veil, he said, voice low and urgent. Keepers of silence. They bury truths to protect their power. But the Spiral... the Spiral is the story they fear most.

Footsteps echoed from the shadows—too many to count—closing in fast.

She pulled you back, whispering, we can't fight them here. Not yet. But if we follow him, we might find the truth buried beneath the city... in the tunnels.

The labyrinth wasn't just metaphor anymore. It was real. Beneath your feet, twisting, alive.

With one last glance at the man, you plunged forward, the cold stone walls closing around you as you entered the underworld of forgotten secrets and buried lies.

The Spiral was no longer just a mystery to solve.

It was a fight to survive.

The tunnels welcomed you with a chilling silence, broken only by the drip of unseen water and the distant echo of hurried footsteps above. The air was thick with dust and something older—forgotten memories pressing against the stone.

The man led you deeper, his pace steady despite the danger. Shadows flickered along the damp walls, painted by the weak glow of a single lantern he carried.

This place, he said, voice rough, "holds what they fear most—a truth that could unravel their control.

She clutched the journal tighter, her eyes scanning the cryptic symbols etched into the walls—signs that matched those in the passage where you found the key.

You could feel it—an ancient power weaving through the labyrinth, pulsing beneath your skin.

Suddenly, the path split.

To the left, the air grew colder, a faint hum resonating from unseen chambers.

To the right, faint voices whispered—fragments of conversations, secrets stolen long ago.

He paused.

The Spiral tests us here. Choose wisely. Every path leads somewhere... but only one leads home.

You looked at her.

She nodded.

The journey was far from over.

And the Spiral's heart was waiting to reveal itself.

It was the key to unlocking the legacy of a hidden world—and the price for uncovering it was only just beginning.

You hesitated, the weight of the choice pressing down like the stones around you. The cold hum to the left called with an eerie calm, promising hidden power or forgotten knowledge. The whispered voices to the right stirred your curiosity—and your fear—like ghosts pleading to be heard.

She stepped forward first, eyes steady. The voices. We need to listen.

Together, you turned down the right path, the whispers growing clearer with each step. Snatches of conversation—a betrayal, a lost child, a hidden ledger—wove through the shadows, a fractured story desperate to be pieced together.

Suddenly, the corridor opened into a cavernous chamber. In its center, a rusted iron chest sat beneath a shaft of pale light filtering through cracks above.

As you approached, the voices faded.

The man from London turned to you both. This chest holds more than secrets. It holds the beginning of everything—the truth that The Veil would kill to keep buried.

She knelt and carefully lifted the heavy lid.

Inside, layers of brittle papers, faded photographs, and a leather-bound book marked with the Spiral's emblem.

Your fingers brushed the book's cover, a chill running through you.

The Spiral was no longer just a path or a puzzle.

As you opened the leather-bound book, the pages whispered beneath your fingertips—fragile, worn, yet alive with ink that seemed to shimmer faintly in the dim light. The script was elegant but unfamiliar, mixing languages and symbols that twisted like the Spiral itself.

She traced a finger over a page filled with sketches: a map of the city intertwined with the labyrinth, marked with cryptic notes and names crossed out in haste.

Look here, she murmured, pointing to a symbol—an eye enclosed in a spiral. This is the mark of The Veil. They've been here, watching, erasing.

The man from London's eyes darkened. And this, he said, is the ledger. It's said to contain the names of those caught in their web—those who tried to unravel the Spiral and disappeared.

Suddenly, the ground trembled—faint at first, then growing stronger.

The Veil was near.

We have to move, she said, closing the book with a snap.

But before you could step back, the chamber's shadows deepened, coalescing into shapes—figures emerging from darkness, silent and imposing.

The Spiral had led you here for a reason.

Now, you had to face the consequence of following its call.

And the fight for truth was no longer a choice.

It was survival.

The figures advanced slowly, their faces obscured by hoods, eyes glinting like cold steel in the low light. The air thickened with tension—every breath a battle against the rising fear.

She clutched the journal, stepping protectively in front of you and the man. They want to keep us silent. But we won't disappear like the others.

The leader raised a hand, and a voice echoed—calm, but edged with menace.

The Spiral is not meant to be unraveled. Some secrets are buried for a reason.

The man from London stepped forward, voice steady. Then you fear the truth more than its consequences. But we carry the light others hide from.

You felt it—something deep inside shifting. The labyrinth, the Spiral, the tangled past and uncertain future—it all converged here, in this moment.

With a sudden burst of resolve, you stepped forward, eyes locked on the shadows.

The Spiral is ours to walk. Not yours to control.

The standoff was fragile, a breath held between darkness and light.

But the journey was far from over.

And the Spiral's pulse beat stronger than ever—calling you forward into the unknown.

A tense silence stretched between you and the hooded figures, broken only by the distant drip of water echoing through the chamber. Then, without warning, the leader lowered their hand, a slow, deliberate motion.

You have courage, the voice said, softer now. But courage alone won't protect you from what lies ahead.

From the shadows, the figures parted, revealing an ancient door carved with spirals and eyes—the very emblem you'd seen in the book. It hummed with an energy that made the air vibrate.

The man from London stepped closer. "This door, he said, is the heart of the labyrinth. Beyond it lies the truth—and the choice that will define everything.

She looked to you, eyes fierce. We've come this far. There's no turning back now.

The leader nodded, as if granting permission.

Together, you approached the door. The key—the same one from the café—glowed faintly in your pocket.

You placed it into the lock.

The Spiral pulsed once more.

The door creaked open.

And the light beyond wasn't what you expected.

It was something new.

Something alive.

Something waiting.

Beyond the door stretched a cavern filled with shimmering light—not harsh or blinding, but warm and breathing, as if the space itself was alive. The walls weren't stone but a swirling mosaic of memories, emotions, and forgotten dreams, shifting in colors you couldn't name.

She stepped forward, her voice barely a whisper. This is the Spiral's core—where past, present, and future intertwine. Here, the truth isn't just seen... it's felt.

The man from London reached out, touching the glowing surface. Images burst forth: faces of those lost, choices made and unmade, paths converged and diverged.

And then—

A single face appeared, clear and steady: the man in the photograph from her mother's purse. Her father.

The realization struck like a thunderclap.

He hadn't vanished. He'd become part of the Spiral itself.

You felt the labyrinth shift beneath your feet, as if welcoming her back, offering answers long denied.

But with every answer came a question:

What price would she—and you—pay to walk the Spiral's path fully?

The journey had revealed its heart.

And now, it demanded everything.

She stepped closer to the glowing image of her father, eyes wide with a mixture of awe and pain.

He's here, she whispered. Not lost... just waiting.

The man from London nodded slowly. "The Spiral holds those who are caught between worlds—between memory and forgetting. Your father's legacy is tied to this place. To the truth The Veil fears.

You felt the weight of that truth settle around you like a cloak—heavy but undeniable.

A sudden pull at your side made you turn.

The journal was glowing now, pages flipping wildly as if alive, revealing a final message in her mother's handwriting:

To find the truth, you must become the Spiral.

The light in the chamber grew brighter, the mosaics swirling faster, drawing you all inward.

Are you ready? she asked, voice steady despite the storm inside.

You looked at the faces in the shifting light—the lost, the hidden, the forgotten—and felt the Spiral calling deep within.

With a breath, you stepped forward together.

Into the unknown.

Into the heart of the labyrinth.

Into the story waiting to be rewritten.

As you stepped forward, the swirling light enveloped you, pulling you deeper into the Spiral's core. The boundaries between past and present blurred—memories, emotions, and secrets merging into a living tapestry that wrapped around your soul.

Her father's face lingered, eyes full of unspoken truths. Around you, fragments of his life flickered—moments stolen from time: laughter, fear, love, and betrayal.

The man from London's voice echoed softly, The Spiral doesn't just hold truth—it tests it. To rewrite the story, you must face what's buried deepest.

Suddenly, a vision seized you: the labyrinth expanding endlessly, paths weaving through shadows and light, choices branching like rivers.

A whisper rose inside your mind, ancient and clear: Every step changes the pattern. Every truth revealed reshapes the Spiral.

She reached for your hand, strength in her grip. We don't just uncover the past. We create the future.

Together, you embraced the pulse of the labyrinth, ready to become the architects of the unknown—to break free from the maze of silence and fear.

Because some mysteries aren't meant to be solved.

They are meant to be lived.

The light around you pulsed like a heartbeat, syncing with your own as the Spiral's energy wove through your veins. Time lost meaning—the labyrinth wasn't just a place anymore, but a living presence, shifting with your every thought and choice.

Suddenly, the mosaic of memories parted, revealing a path—a luminous thread winding deeper into the heart of the Spiral. It was both invitation and challenge.

She looked at you, eyes fierce with determination. This is where the real journey begins. Beyond here, the Spiral will test everything we believe—our fears, our hopes, even our very identities.

The man from London stepped forward, voice low. Those who walk this path risk losing themselves... but also gain the power to change the story forever.

You took a breath, feeling the weight of all that had led you here—and all that awaited.

With a final glance at each other, you stepped onto the glowing thread.

The labyrinth embraced you, not as prisoners, but as creators.

And in that moment, you understood:

The Spiral is not a maze to escape.

It is the dance of becoming—

of facing the unknown,

and forging light from shadow.

Your story was no longer written for you.

It was yours to write.

The path beneath your feet pulsed with radiant energy, guiding you deeper into the Spiral's heart. With every step, the walls around you shifted—now familiar faces appeared, now distant echoes of laughter and tears intertwined.

She whispered, we carry their stories... their unfinished journeys. To move forward, we must honor them.

The man from London nodded, eyes sharp. And confront the darkness they feared. Only then can we reshape the Spiral's course.

Ahead, the thread of light led to a chamber where time seemed suspended. In its center stood a mirror—tall, ornate, and shimmering with a soft, otherworldly glow.

The final test, she said.

You approached, heart pounding.

The mirror didn't show your reflection. Instead, it revealed a convergence—a tapestry of choices, mistakes, love, and loss. Each thread glowed with possibility.

To step through was to accept the Spiral fully—to embrace all that was known and unknown, to weave your own path in the endless dance.

The air thickened with quiet anticipation.

You looked at her.

She smiled, a spark of hope.

Together, you reached out—

ready to step beyond reflection,

beyond fear,

into the boundless spiral of becoming.

Your fingers brushed the mirror's surface, and the world rippled like water. The threads of the tapestry pulled you forward, weaving your essence into the Spiral's endless flow.

For a moment, everything dissolved—time, space, identity—all melting into one luminous pulse.

Then, clarity.

You were no longer just a traveler in the labyrinth.

You were part of it.

The stories you carried, the secrets you uncovered, and the love and loss intertwined became a new pattern—a living thread in the Spiral's design.

She stood beside you, eyes shining with the same light now glowing from within.

The man from London nodded solemnly. We've become the keepers. The creators. The story itself.

As the chamber faded, the Spiral opened before you—no longer a maze to escape, but a path to build.

And somewhere, deep within that endless design, a face smiled—the father, the lost, the found—waiting for the next step.

You breathed in the mystery, knowing this was only the beginning.

Because some journeys never end.

They only spiral onward.

As the light softened, the three of you stood together—no longer bound by doubt or fear, but united by purpose. The labyrinth had transformed from a prison of secrets into a canvas of possibility.

She turned to you, voice steady yet full of wonder.

We carry more than answers now. We carry hope.

The man from London added, The Spiral will keep changing, shifting with every choice we make. It's alive—like us.

You felt it, too—the pulse of infinite paths stretching out, inviting creation over escape.

A new door appeared, carved not with spirals, but with open hands reaching outward.

It's time, you said, to walk forward—not as seekers lost, but as makers of our own story.

Together, you stepped through.

Into the light of the unknown,

the embrace of mystery,

and the endless dance of becoming.

The face you once saw wasn't an ending.

It was the spark that lit the Spiral's fire.

And now, it was yours to keep burning.

Beyond the door, the world shifted once more—a place where memories and futures intertwined like threads of light and shadow. Here, the Spiral was not just a path, but a living storybook, waiting to be written with each step you took.

She smiled, the weight of the past now softened by the promise of what lay ahead.

This is our beginning, she said. Not just to uncover, but to create.

The man from London nodded, his eyes reflecting the swirling light.

We're no longer chasing ghosts. We're shaping destiny.

You felt the journal in your hand, its pages now blank but alive with possibility.

With a deep breath, you opened it and wrote the first line of this new chapter:

In the labyrinth of shadows, we found the light to build our own path.

And as the Spiral pulsed gently beneath your feet, you stepped forward—ready to face whatever mysteries awaited, together.

The air around you shimmered with promise, the unknown no longer a source of fear but a wellspring of possibility. The labyrinth, once a maze of secrets and shadows, now felt like an invitation—a living map drawn by your own choices.

She squeezed your hand. Every step from here will reshape not only the Spiral, but who we are.

The man from London smiled faintly, eyes reflecting the endless paths unfolding before you. And somewhere in this endless dance, we'll find the peace we've been searching for.

You closed the journal gently, feeling its warmth settle like a pulse against your palm.

The Spiral's light stretched before you—no longer a trap, but a path of becoming, endlessly winding, endlessly new.

Together, you walked on.

Because some faces we see once

are the ones that guide us forever.

And some stories—like the Spiral—never truly end.

They only begin again.

As you walked deeper into the Spiral's glow, the labyrinth around you shifted once more, revealing glimpses of places and people you had yet to meet. The threads of your story intertwined with countless others, each step weaving new patterns of hope, loss, and discovery.

She looked ahead, her eyes bright with quiet determination.

This is more than a journey, she said softly. It's a promise—to ourselves, to those we've lost, and to the future we choose to build.

The man from London nodded, his voice steady.

Whatever comes next, we face it together. As keepers of the Spiral, as creators of our own fate.

You took a deep breath, feeling the weight and freedom of the moment.

The Spiral pulsed beneath your feet—alive, infinite, and waiting.

And in that eternal dance, you found your place.

The face you saw once was never just a memory.

It was a beginning.

The light around you softened, and the labyrinth's pulse slowed to a steady rhythm, like a heartbeat in sync with your own. Each step forward was both an ending and a promise—a reminder that the Spiral was never about escape, but about transformation.

She turned to you, a quiet smile touching her lips.

We're no longer bound by the past. The Spiral's story is ours now.

The man from London looked toward the horizon of shifting paths.

Every choice we make writes new lines, new faces, new futures.

You felt the journal's weight in your hand—a vessel of infinite possibility.

With resolve, you opened it again and wrote:

In the endless spiral, we become the light that guides others home.

Together, you stepped into the unfolding journey—where mystery meets courage, and every ending sparks a new beginning.

Because some faces we glimpse once

ignite a fire that burns forever.

The Spiral stretched endlessly before you, its winding paths alive with whispers of untold stories and hidden truths. You felt the weight of the journey behind you, but more powerfully, the promise of what lay ahead.

She took a deep breath, eyes reflecting the labyrinth's glow.

"This is our legacy—not just to uncover the past, but to forge the future."

The man from London smiled, a hint of peace in his gaze.

"The Spiral doesn't trap us. It frees us, when we dare to step into the unknown."

You closed the journal gently, feeling the warmth of countless possibilities ripple through your fingertips.

Together, you walked forward, the Spiral's light guiding you—
not as lost souls,
but as creators of a story still unfolding.
Because some faces are more than memories.
They are the first spark of every new dawn.

The labyrinth's glow softened into a warm embrace, wrapping around you like a quiet promise. Each step forward felt lighter—as if the weight of uncertainty was transforming into the power of choice.

She glanced at you, eyes shimmering with a new kind of strength.

We've come through the maze, but the journey is just beginning. The Spiral lives in us now.

The man from London nodded, his voice steady but hopeful.

Every secret we've uncovered, every shadow faced, has shaped who we are—and who we will become.

You felt the journal pulse softly in your hands, its pages ready to receive the next chapter.

Together, you stepped into the unfolding light,
carrying the face you once saw like a beacon—
a guide through darkness,
a call to create meaning from mystery.

Because in the Spiral of life, every end is just the start of something greater.

As you moved forward, the labyrinth seemed to breathe with you—each twist and turn alive with possibility. The Spiral no longer whispered warnings but sang with promise, weaving your story into its eternal dance.

She reached out, her hand finding yours.

We're not just walking paths anymore. We're shaping them.

The man from London smiled, a rare softness breaking through.

Somewhere in the maze, we lost fear and found purpose.

The journal, now a living map of your journey, glowed faintly—its pages waiting for your next words.

With steady breath, you began to write:

In the heart of the Spiral, we become the storytellers of our own destiny.

Together, you embraced the unknown ahead—ready to face whatever mysteries, wonders, and challenges the Spiral would bring.

Because some faces, once seen, become the compass guiding us through every labyrinth we face.

The path ahead shimmered with possibility, each step echoing with the pulse of the Spiral beneath your feet. The labyrinth's walls, once cold and confining, now seemed to hum with life—inviting, expansive, alive.

She squeezed your hand gently.

We're no longer wandering. We're creating.

The man from London looked toward the shifting horizon.

The past was a shadow, but the future is light—waiting to be shaped.

The journal's pages fluttered open, blank yet brimming with silent potential.

You lifted your pen, heart steady, mind clear.

Here, in the endless spiral, we choose our story—and with each choice, we become more than who we were.

And together, you stepped forward—

into the labyrinth that was no longer a maze,

but a journey without end,

a story without final page,

a spiral ever turning toward light.

The light around you deepened into a calm glow, wrapping the three of you in a quiet sanctuary within the endless Spiral. The echoes of the past no longer haunted but whispered encouragement — a reminder that every step forward was a choice, a creation.

She looked to you, eyes steady and fierce.

We carry their stories, yes. But now, we add our own.

The man from London nodded slowly, a softness breaking through his guarded exterior.

The Spiral isn't just a path to walk. It's a legacy to leave.

You closed the journal gently, feeling the weight of that legacy settle like a flame within your chest.

Ahead, the Spiral stretched out — infinite, inviting, alive.

And in that infinite dance of shadows and light, you understood.

Some faces we see once

are the compass that guides us through every twist, every turn.

And some stories — like the Spiral —

are meant to be lived, again and again,

each time a little brighter, a little wiser,

a little more whole.

The Spiral's glow pulsed softly, as if breathing alongside you. The labyrinth had shifted from a place of fear and confusion into a realm of possibility and renewal.

She stepped forward, her voice steady but filled with hope.

We were lost once, but now we're found — not by escaping the maze, but by becoming part of its story.

The man from London smiled softly, a rare peace settling over him.

The Spiral connects us all—past, present, and future. We're part of something greater now.

You felt the journal warm in your hands, its pages waiting patiently for the next chapter.

With a steady breath, you began to write:

In the heart of mystery, we find our true selves — not in the answers, but in the courage to keep seeking.

And as the Spiral pulsed beneath your feet, you stepped forward —

into the unknown,

into the story still unfolding,

into the endless dance of light and shadow.

The Spiral's light stretched before you like an uncharted sky, vast and shimmering with untold stories. Each step forward was a step deeper into the unknown—and yet, the fear that once gripped you had softened into something else: a fierce, quiet curiosity.

She looked at you both, her voice barely more than a whisper.

We are no longer prisoners of the past. We are architects of what comes next.

The man from London looked ahead, the weight of his past lightened by the promise of what lies ahead.

The maze is not a prison—it's a path to becoming.

You opened the journal once more, its pages glowing softly, ready to receive your truth.

With deliberate calm, you wrote:

In the dance of shadows and light, we are both lost and found—always moving forward, always becoming more.

And as the Spiral spiraled onward, so did you—

into the mystery,

into the light,

into the story still waiting to be told.

The air around you thickened with quiet anticipation, the labyrinth's pulse syncing with your own heartbeat. The Spiral was no longer a puzzle to solve but a living story to inhabit—one that would stretch beyond time, beyond fear.

She reached out, tracing a line in the air that shimmered into existence—an invisible thread connecting past, present, and future.

"We don't just walk the labyrinth. We weave it.

The man from London's eyes gleamed with newfound clarity.

The face you saw once—it was never just a memory. It was a call.

The journal opened before you, blank pages filled with endless possibility.

You raised your pen, the weight of your choice settling like a steady flame.

This spiral we walk is not a cage but a compass—leading us toward the light we carry within.

Together, you stepped into the unknown—ready to write the next chapter, to face the shadows, and to embrace the endless spiral of becoming.

The labyrinth seemed to breathe around you, walls shifting softly like the pages of a living book. Each step was both a question and an answer, a thread woven tighter into the tapestry of your unfolding story.

She looked at you, her voice steady as the Spiral's rhythm.

We've carried the past long enough. Now, we carry possibility.

The man from London nodded, a quiet strength settling in his gaze.

The face you saw once—it's a key. Not just to who we were, but to who we can be.

The journal glowed warmly in your hands, waiting.

You lifted your pen, heart steady.

In the spiral's endless dance, we find not only our history, but our hope.

And as you wrote, the labyrinth opened before you—

not as a maze to escape, but a path to transform.

The Spiral's glow deepened, casting long shadows that danced like whispers along the labyrinth's walls. The air hummed with secrets waiting to be spoken, promises waiting to be kept.

She stepped closer, her fingers grazing the surface of the journal as if drawing strength from its pages.

We're more than seekers now. We're storytellers, builders of what comes next.

The man from London inhaled deeply, his eyes reflecting the labyrinth's endless curves.

The face you saw once—it's a reminder. That even in darkness, there's light to be found, paths to be chosen.

You felt the weight of the moment settle like a quiet fire in your chest. Pen poised, you wrote:

In every twist of the Spiral, there is a choice—to fear or to hope, to hide or to become.

Together, you stepped forward, the labyrinth welcoming you—not as prisoners, but as creators of a story still unfolding,

a dance between shadow and light,

between the known and the infinite unknown.

The labyrinth around you seemed to pulse with life, its walls breathing stories into the air like whispered secrets. Every shadow held a question; every light a promise.

She turned to you, her gaze steady, unwavering.

We don't follow the Spiral anymore. We shape it.

The man from London nodded, a faint smile breaking the weight of his past.

The face you saw once... it's not just a memory. It's a beginning.

The journal glowed faintly, pages fluttering as if eager for what comes next.

You raised your pen, feeling the gravity of the moment—of choices yet to be made.

In the Spiral's endless turning, we find the courage not to escape, but to become.

And with that, you stepped deeper—into the unknown, into the story only you could write.

The Spiral's light shimmered, casting ripples across the labyrinth like the surface of a restless sea. Each step forward felt both familiar and new, as if the maze itself was alive—breathing, watching, waiting.

She reached out, her fingers brushing a shimmering thread that wove through the air.

This thread, she whispered, is the path we choose. Not the one given, but the one we create.

The man from London's eyes glinted with a quiet fire.

The face you saw once was never just a ghost of the past—it's the spark that ignites what's yet to come.

The journal's pages turned slowly, inviting you to write the next line, the next truth.

You steadied your breath, pen poised above paper.

In the heart of the Spiral, where shadows meet light, we find not endings, but beginnings.

Together, you stepped forward—into the unfolding story,

into the labyrinth made not of walls, but of choices,

into the endless dance of becoming.

The labyrinth seemed to pulse in response, walls shimmering with faint echoes of footsteps yet to come. The Spiral wasn't just beneath your feet—it was within you, winding through memory and hope, fear and courage.

She looked at you both, her voice low but certain.

We're no longer chasing shadows. We're making light.

The man from London took a slow breath, eyes bright with unspoken resolve.

The face you saw once—it's the thread that ties us all. The lost, the found, and those still searching.

The journal lay open, waiting patiently for your hand to guide it.

5: The Spiral as a symbol of memory, fate, and rebirth

With quiet certainty, you wrote:

Within the Spiral's endless loops, we discover not just who we were—but who we choose to become.

And as your words settled on the page, the labyrinth shifted—no longer a maze, but a gateway,

leading you onward into the vast unknown,

where every step was a promise,

and every turn a new beginning.

The air thickened with possibility, the labyrinth's pulse growing steady—an unspoken invitation to move forward, to step beyond what was known. The Spiral was no longer a maze of fear, but a map of becoming.

She smiled softly, eyes glinting with quiet strength.

We're the authors now. Every choice, every step—our story.

The face you saw once was never just a memory. It's a beacon.

The journal hummed in your hands, pages glowing with uncharted futures.

You dipped your pen in resolve and wrote:

In the Spiral's dance, we embrace the unknown—not as a threat, but as a promise.

The labyrinth's walls pulsed gently, alive with whispers from the past and echoes of the future. The Spiral beneath your feet was no longer a trap, but a guide—a rhythm syncing with your own heartbeat.

She reached out, fingers brushing the air as if pulling threads from unseen corners.

We walk not just for answers, but for transformation.

The man from London's gaze softened, shadows lifting from his eyes.

The face you saw once isn't just a fragment—it's a bridge.

The journal's pages shimmered, inviting the next step.

With steady hands, you wrote:

Through every twist and turn, we unravel the mystery within ourselves.

And as the Spiral stretched before you, you stepped forward—
not into uncertainty,
but into the light of becoming.

The Spiral glowed brighter now, its rhythm pulsing like a living heartbeat beneath your feet. The labyrinth was no longer a maze of confusion—it was a symphony of possibilities, each note a choice, each step a new verse.

She turned to you, eyes reflecting the endless curves ahead.

We don't just seek the path anymore. We shape it with every breath.

The man from London exhaled slowly, the weight of his past lifting like morning mist.

The face you saw once—it's a key, not to the past, but to what lies beyond.

The journal in your hands warmed, pages fluttering as if eager to be written.

You dipped your pen with purpose and inscribed:

In the Spiral's endless dance, we find our truth—not in endings, but in the courage to continue.

The journal lay open, glowing softly, waiting for the next chapter.

With steady breath, you wrote:

Within the Spiral's endless turning, we find the strength to become the story we were always meant to tell.

And as your words settled, the labyrinth shifted—
not a trap, but a passage—
leading you forward, deeper into the light of what is yet to be.

The Spiral's glow thickened, wrapping around you like a living pulse—an ancient rhythm beating in time with your own. The labyrinth no longer whispered secrets; it shouted truths, demanding you listen, demanding you move.

The journal's pages flared bright, the words begging to be written, the truth demanding release.

She stepped closer, voice steady, eyes fierce.

Every step burns the old away.

It's a warning. A call. A reckoning.

The journal's pages blazed with light, waiting for your hand to write the truth that could no longer be ignored.

You gripped your pen like a weapon and wrote:

In the Spiral's relentless turning, we find the power not to escape, but to confront—to become.

The labyrinth roared around you—walls bending, time twisting—

and you stepped forward, not just into the unknown,

but into the fire of your own becoming.

She met your gaze, eyes burning with fierce determination.

We don't run from the Spiral. We own it. Every twist is ours to command.

With iron resolve, you gripped your pen and wrote:

In the heart of the Spiral, we choose not submission, but mastery—rising from the shadows to claim our story.

And as the labyrinth shattered around you, reality bent and cracked—

you stepped forward, blazing into the unknown,

reborn in fire and light, unstoppable.

The walls trembled, ancient stones shifting as the labyrinth responded to your will. The Spiral's glow became a roaring blaze, illuminating paths unseen and truths long buried.

She reached out, her voice a fierce command.

This is our crucible. We don't break—we become stronger in the flames.

With every ounce of strength, you wrote:

In the Spiral's fire, we are forged anew—no longer shadows, but the architects of our fate.

And as the labyrinth bowed to your resolve, the path forward ignited—

leading you beyond fear, beyond memory,

into the uncharted brilliance of what lies ahead.

The path before you burned with fierce light, every step a declaration—a refusal to be bound by the past's chains. The labyrinth, once cold and twisting, now thrummed with raw energy, alive with the power of choice.

She turned to you both, voice steady as steel.

This is not just survival. It's transformation. The Spiral demands nothing less.

And as the labyrinth opened wide, you stepped forward—
into the unknown,
into the light,
into the story only you could write.

The labyrinth's walls seemed to breathe around you, the Spiral's pulse now a steady drumbeat echoing deep within your bones. It was no longer a place of confusion but a crucible—a forge for the soul.

She reached out, fingers tracing invisible patterns in the air.

This journey isn't about finding answers outside ourselves. It's about awakening what's always been inside.

With calm certainty, you wrote:

In the heart of the Spiral, the labyrinth becomes a path—not to escape, but to discover the courage to face ourselves.

And with that, the maze unfolded before you—not as a prison, but as a gateway—leading you onward, deeper into light and truth.

6: Ariadne's Thread

The myth of Theseus and the Minotaur on Crete is the perfect ancient echo: a hero venturing into the maze to face a terrifying beast, navigating twists and turns to find truth and survival.

Ariadne's thread weaving with Theseus's story adds layers—linking the modern mystery to timeless human struggles with fear, identity, and courage. The labyrinth becomes not just a physical space but a metaphor for facing inner demons and ancestral shadows, the dark sides of history and self.

The weight of the labyrinth's legacy settled over you like a shroud. This was no ordinary maze—it was a living myth, pulsing with echoes of Crete, Theseus, and the monstrous Minotaur lurking in the shadows of time.

Ariandne's thread intertwined with the ancient tale, a modern Theseus tasked with facing the darkness not just outside—but within. The Spiral beneath your feet was both path and prison, a test of courage where each turn could bring salvation or destruction.

She whispered, voice low but fierce,

Every labyrinth holds a beast. Not always outside—sometimes inside us, in the places we fear to look.

The man from London clenched his fists, the face in the portrait burning behind his eyes.

The Minotaur isn't just a monster. It's the legacy we inherit—the violence, the secrets, the silence. We have to face it, or be consumed.

The journal trembled, pages flickering with ancient symbols and modern scripts—calling you to write the final chapter.

You took a deep breath and began:

Like Theseus, we enter the labyrinth not to conquer a monster, but to reclaim the light stolen by fear and shadows.

The Spiral pulsed faster, a heartbeat of destiny—inviting you forward into myth, into memory, into the fight to transform darkness into light.

The deeper you stepped into the Spiral, the more the labyrinth revealed itself—not just stone and shadow, but a living tapestry woven with threads of myth and memory. The walls seemed to breathe stories long forgotten, whispers of those who dared to face their monsters.

She turned, eyes burning with conviction.

This labyrinth is more than a place. It's a journey into the soul—where the Minotaur waits not just in the dark corners, but in the fear we refuse to name.

Ariadne's voice broke through the silence, steady but charged.

The beast's power comes from the silence around it—the secrets, the untold stories, the broken connections. To defeat it, we must bring light to all that's hidden.

The man from London's gaze hardened, the portrait's face no longer just an enigma, but a challenge etched into his bloodline.

The labyrinth demands truth. Only by embracing the past can we shape the future.

The journal's pages shimmered with energy, eager for your hand to write the next truth.

With steady breath, you inscribed:

In the heart of the labyrinth, the monster is not our enemy—but the shadow we must accept to become whole.

And as the Spiral's light swelled around you, the path forward opened wide—no longer a prison, but a passage into transformation, into the courage to face whatever lies within.

With the words written, a tremor rippled through the labyrinth, shaking loose dust and shadows long settled. The Spiral's pulse grew louder—a steady drum calling you deeper into the maze, where light and darkness intertwined.

She reached out, her hand brushing a carved stone—ancient symbols igniting with a faint glow.

This is the language of those who walked before us. They faced their monsters too. They left clues, if we dare to see.

Ariadne's eyes flickered with newfound resolve.

The Minotaur's roar isn't just fear—it's a call to awaken. To claim what's been lost.

The man from London stepped forward, the face in his eyes no longer distant but alive with purpose.

We are the thread between past and future, the line that weaves the labyrinth's meaning.

The journal lay open, waiting.

You gripped the pen once more, heart pounding, and wrote:

The labyrinth is not a cage but a canvas—each step a stroke, each fear a color. To navigate it is to paint our own salvation.

The Spiral glowed fiercely, the path unfolding—

leading you onward, deeper into the mystery,

closer to the light beyond the shadow.

The air thickened as the Spiral's glow pulsed in sync with your heartbeat. Every step forward felt heavier, yet somehow freer—as if the labyrinth itself was testing your resolve, daring you to unravel its deepest secrets.

She paused at a narrow corridor, where faded frescoes hinted at a story half-told.

Look closely, she urged, "the past isn't just history—it's a warning, and a key.

Armando studied the symbols carved into the walls, tracing their curves with a trembling finger.

These marks... they speak of a price paid. Of sacrifices made to keep the beast bound.

The man from London's jaw clenched.

But the binding weakened long ago. That face we saw—the one hidden in shadows—he wasn't just hunted. He was a prisoner of his own choices.

You felt the journal pulse again, as if alive, urging you to write the truth lurking beneath the surface.

With determination, you wrote:

To face the labyrinth's monster, we must first face ourselves—the fears, the regrets, the truths we bury deepest.

And as your words took shape, the labyrinth responded—walls shifting, light bending, and the path ahead revealing a door carved with the same spiral that had led you here.

Beyond it lay the final reckoning:

a confrontation with the past, the monster, and the chance to rewrite the story once and for all.

Your hand trembled as you reached for the door, the carved spiral seeming to pulse beneath your fingertips like a heartbeat. The air beyond whispered promises and threats, tangled in the same breath.

She looked at you, eyes fierce and steady.

This is where the maze stops being a puzzle—and becomes a choice.

Armando's voice was low, haunted.

The man in the portrait... he lived with the monster inside. But maybe, just maybe, he left us the means to tame it.

The man from London nodded slowly, his gaze fixed on the door.

To face what's behind this door is to face the legacy we all carry—the darkness, the secrets, and the hope.

You felt the weight of

the journal in your hands—more than paper, it was a lifeline. With a steady breath, you pushed the door open.

Inside, shadows danced against flickering torchlight, and at the center, a figure stood—half-hidden, half-revealed. The face you saw once, now unmistakably alive.

The labyrinth held its breath.

And so did you.

The figure stepped forward, the flickering light catching the sharp lines of a face both familiar a foreign—worn by time, but burning with quiet intensity.

I've waited, the man said, voice rough but steady. Not just for you... but for the moment the past could be faced without fear.

She swallowed hard, recognition flickering in her eyes.

Why did you disappear? Why leave us in shadows?

He looked away, pain threading through his gaze.

The labyrinth isn't just stone and myth. It's a burden—a price for the choices I made. But it's also a chance to break free.

Armando stepped closer, eyes narrowing.

What price? What choices?

The man's hands clenched, trembling.

I was trapped between two worlds—the trader and the monster, the father and the stranger. I carried secrets too heavy to bear alone.

You tightened your grip on the journal, heart pounding. This was the moment—the crossroads where truth and legend collided.

He met your eyes, voice soft but unwavering.

The face you saw once... it's not just mine. It's the face of every fear we hide. But it's also the face of redemption.

The labyrinth breathed around you, waiting for your next move.

The silence stretched, thick and heavy, as if the labyrinth itself was holding its breath. You felt the weight of countless untold stories pressing in—echoes of pain, loss, and hope tangled together like the roots beneath the maze.

She stepped forward, voice steady yet gentle.

So, the labyrinth wasn't meant to trap you... but to protect us? To protect the truth?

He nodded slowly, shadows flickering across his face.

Exactly. Some secrets are prisons, but some are shields. I disappeared because the darkness chasing me could have destroyed everything—our family, our past, our future.

Armando's gaze sharpened, searching for the answers beneath the sorrow.

"What must we do now? How do we face what's coming?

The man's eyes glinted with quiet fire.

We walk the labyrinth together. We face the beast, not as enemies, but as fragments of the same story. Only then can the Spiral unwind, and the light break through.

You opened the journal once more, fingers trembling, and wrote:

The labyrinth's end is not defeat—it is union. In facing the darkness within, we find the strength to rewrite our fate.

The door behind you closed softly, sealing the past.

Ahead, the path glimmered with promise—and the first true dawn of understanding.

The flickering torchlight revealed a narrow corridor beyond the chamber, its walls inscribed with symbols that seemed to pulse with ancient energy. The air was thick with anticipation—every step forward felt like peeling back layers of time itself.

She glanced at you, eyes sharp with resolve.

This is the heart of the labyrinth—the place where all threads converge. What we face now will change everything.

Armando pulled a small, worn object from his pocket—a pendant shaped like a spiral, matching the labyrinth's pattern.

My grandfather gave this to me. He said it's a guide, but only if we're ready to see the truth.

The man from London traced the symbols on the wall.

These markings tell a story of sacrifice and hope, of a beast that wasn't just a monster, but a mirror.

You felt the journal pulse again, the pages warm beneath your fingertips, as if alive with possibility.

Taking a deep breath, you stepped forward, the spiral pendant glowing faintly in your hand.

The labyrinth was no longer just a mystery—it was a path to redemption. And the story was yours to finish.

With each step, deeper into the labyrinth, the symbols on the walls grew clearer—now glowing softly, illuminating a path that twisted and turned like a living thing. The spiral pendant pulsed in your hand, guiding you as if it held the heartbeat of the maze itself.

With each step, the corridor seemed to shift—walls breathing in rhythm with your pulse, the symbols glowing brighter, guiding you deeper into the labyrinth's heart. The spiral pendant in your hand thrummed softly, a steady beacon amid the growing darkness.

She whispered, "It's like the labyrinth knows us... understands our fears, our hopes."

Armando nodded. Every story etched here is a warning and a promise. The beast we fear is the shadow of what we refuse to face.

The man from London's voice was steady but laced with emotion.

This is more than a journey. It's a reckoning. The face you saw once... it's a call to confront the legacy that binds us.

Ahead, a faint light shimmered—fragile, yet unwavering.

You opened the journal, and the pages began to fill with words unspoken, memories unclaimed, futures unwritten.

You wrote,

In the labyrinth's darkest folds, we find the light we thought lost. The beast is not our enemy—it is the key.

The spiral's glow expanded, wrapping around you like a cloak of truth.

The final chamber awaited.

And with it, the choice to break the cycle—or become part of the maze forever.

She whispered, this isn't just a maze of stone. It's a map of the soul. Every turn reveals a truth we need to confront.

Armando's voice was steady but filled with awe.

The beast we fear is the reflection of what we refuse to face—the darkness inside us all.

The man from London stopped and looked back, eyes heavy with memory.

My father vanished here, trapped by his own demons. I thought I was chasing a ghost,

but maybe... I was chasing myself.

The journal pages fluttered, revealing a new passage, as if responding to the energy in the air:

To walk the labyrinth is to accept the shadows within, to hold both fear and hope in one hand. Only then can the Spiral open to the light beyond.

You looked ahead, the path narrowing into a final chamber bathed in a soft, ethereal glow.

The moment had come—to face the labyrinth's heart, and the truth it guarded.

With each step, the corridor seemed to shift—walls breathing in rhythm with your pulse, the symbols glowing brighter, guiding you deeper into the labyrinth's heart. The spiral pendant in your hand thrummed softly, a steady beacon amid the growing darkness.

She whispered, it's like the labyrinth knows us... understands our fears, our hopes.

Armando nodded. Every story etched here is a warning and a promise. The beast we fear is the shadow of what we refuse to face.

The man from London's voice was steady but laced with emotion.

This is more than a journey. It's a reckoning. The face you saw once... it's a call to confront the legacy that binds us.

Ahead, a faint light shimmered—fragile, yet unwavering.

You opened the journal, and the pages began to fill with words unspoken, memories unclaimed, futures unwritten.

You wrote,

In the labyrinth's darkest folds, we find the light we thought lost. The beast is not our enemy—it is the key.

The spiral's glow expanded, wrapping around you like a cloak of truth.

The final chamber awaited.

And with it, the choice to break the cycle—or become part of the maze forever.

The light grew steadier as you approached the chamber's entrance—a vast archway carved with intricate spirals that seemed to pulse with life. The air was thick with anticipation, the silence broken only by the soft hum of the pendant resting in your palm.

She looked at you, eyes fierce and unblinking.

This is it. The heart of the labyrinth. The place where truth and shadow collide.

Armando took a deep breath.

The man in the portrait—your friend's father—he lived trapped in this very conflict. Now, it's our turn to finish what was started.

The man from London stepped forward, his voice low but certain.

To face the beast, we must face ourselves. The labyrinth doesn't just test strength—it tests the courage to forgive, to accept, to change.

You felt the journal's pages flutter, as if urging you onward.

With a shared glance, the four of you crossed the threshold.

Inside, the chamber unfolded like a living story—walls alive with flickering images, memories replaying in a dance of light and shadow.

As the spiral of light enveloped the chamber, the Minotaur's form began to dissolve—no longer a beast, but a man freed from the shadows of his past. The heavy weight of sorrow lifted, replaced by a quiet peace that settled over you all.

She stepped closer to the fading figure, tears glistening in her eyes.

"So this is what he wanted all along—a chance to be seen, to be understood."

Armando exhaled slowly, the pendant's glow dimming to a gentle pulse.

"The labyrinth wasn't just his prison. It was his plea for connection, for forgiveness."

The man from London lowered his head, a mixture of relief and grief in his voice.

"Now that we've faced him, we can begin to heal the wounds he left behind."

You closed the journal, the final page inscribed with a single line:

"In embracing the darkness within, we discover the light that guides us home."

The labyrinth's walls shimmered and faded, revealing a doorway bathed in warm morning light.

Stepping through it, you felt the weight of the past lift, replaced by the promise of a future reclaimed—not just for you, but for all who walk the spiral path.

The story had found its end.

But the journey was only beginning.

And at the center, the Minotaur—half-man, half-beast—stood waiting. Not a monster to slay, but a reflection.

The labyrinth had one last secret to reveal:

to escape, you had to embrace the beast within.

The Minotaur's eyes locked onto yours, not with rage, but with profound sadness—as if it carried the weight of every hidden pain, every shattered hope.

She stepped forward, voice steady but soft.

It's not a monster. It's a guardian... a mirror of what we fear to see.

Armando's hand tightened around the spiral pendant, the glow pulsing in response.

To break the cycle, we don't fight the beast—we understand it.

The man from London nodded.

He was my father. And in his torment, he became this labyrinth's shadow. But he's also our link to the truth we've been chasing.

You felt the journal warm in your hands, pages now filled with stories of courage, loss, and redemption.

You breathed deeply and spoke aloud:

We accept you—not as enemy, but as part of us. The darkness and light, entwined.

The chamber trembled, the flickering images merging into a brilliant spiral of light.

The labyrinth was no longer a prison.

It was a passage—leading not into darkness, but into a new dawn.

As the spiral of light enveloped the chamber, the Minotaur's form began to dissolve—no longer a beast, but a man freed from the shadows of his past. The heavy weight of sorrow lifted, replaced by a quiet peace that settled over you all.

She stepped closer to the fading figure, tears glistening in her eyes.

So, this is what he wanted all along—a chance to be seen, to be understood.

Armando exhaled slowly, the pendant's glow dimming to a gentle pulse.

The labyrinth wasn't just his prison. It was his plea for connection, for forgiveness.

The man from London lowered his head, the air buzzed softly with possibility, as if the labyrinth's breath had been exhaled at last. You felt the weight of the past lighten, replaced by a quiet determination.

She looked at you, eyes bright with newfound clarity.

The spiral isn't just a symbol of what traps us—it's the shape of how we grow.

Armando adjusted the pendant, now resting calmly around his neck.

We carry our stories with us, but they don't have to define us.

The man from London smiled, a fragile peace settling over him.

Maybe the greatest mystery isn't who we are... but who we choose to become.

Together, you stepped away from the labyrinth's shadow, the city waking around you like a promise.

And somewhere deep inside, the spiral pulsed—not as a chain, but as a compass, leading always onward.

The journey was far from over.

It had just begun. mixture of relief and grief in his voice.

Now that we've faced him, we can begin to heal the wounds he left behind.

You closed the journal, the final page inscribed with a single line:

In embracing the darkness within, we discover the light that guides us home.

The labyrinth's walls shimmered and faded, revealing a doorway bathed in warm morning light.

Stepping through it, you felt the weight of the past lift, replaced by the promise of a future reclaimed—not just for you, but for all who walk the spiral path.

The story had found its end.

But the journey was only beginning.

Beyond the doorway, the world felt reborn—colors sharper, air lighter, and the sky stretched wide with endless possibility. The labyrinth's grip had loosened, but its lessons echoed in every heartbeat.

She turned to you, a quiet smile breaking through the shadows.

We came searching for answers... but what we found was far more.

Armando nodded, eyes reflecting the morning light.

A path forward. Not just for us, but for those still lost in their own spirals.

The man from London held the spiral pendant tightly, as if passing on a silent vow.

Redemption isn't a destination. It's a choice we make every day.

You opened the journal one last time, pages now blank but alive with potential.

With steady hands, you wrote:

The face I saw once is no longer a mystery—but a mirror. A reminder that every labyrinth holds a way out, if we dare to walk it.

As the sun climbed higher, you stepped forward—into the unknown, ready to write the next chapter.

You felt the weight of the past lighten, replaced by a quiet determination.

She looked at you, eyes bright with newfound clarity.

The spiral isn't just a symbol of what traps us—it's the shape of how we grow.

Armando adjusted the pendant, now resting calmly around his neck.

We carry our stories with us, but they don't have to define us.

Together, you stepped away from the labyrinth's shadow, the city waking around you like a promise.

And somewhere deep inside, the spiral pulsed—not as a chain, but as a compass, leading always onward.

The journey was far from over.

It had just begun.

Days turned into weeks, and the threads of the labyrinth began to weave into the fabric of your everyday life. The mystery had unfolded, but its echoes lingered—quiet reminders that some journeys don't end, they evolve.

She approached you one evening, holding a small, folded map—ancient and worn, yet marked with the same spiral symbol.

This isn't just a memory. It's a guide. Another labyrinth, waiting.

Armando traced the lines with a steady finger.

Different place,

different time. But the same story: secrets buried, truths waiting to breathe.

The man from London looked up, eyes sharp.

And this time, we're not just walking the path—we're shaping it.

You felt the journal pulse faintly at your side, as if eager for new pages to be written.

With a shared breath, you all stepped forward once more—into the next great unknown.

Because some faces we see once,

stay with us forever.

And some labyrinths never truly end.

The map led you beyond city streets, into forgotten corners where history whispered beneath cracked stone and tangled ivy. Each step echoed the past—footprints of those who'd walked before, lost or found.

She paused at a weathered archway carved with the same spiral, now worn by time but no less potent.

This place... it feels alive. Like the labyrinth grew, shifted.

Armando's eyes narrowed.

Not just a place. A memory. A warning.

The man from London fingered a faded inscription on the wall—words half-erased but charged with meaning.

To find the face, you must become the mirror.

You felt the weight of the phrase settle deep inside you.

The journey ahead wasn't just about uncovering secrets.

It was about becoming the story—transforming mystery into meaning, shadow into light.

And somewhere, beyond the next bend, the spiral pulsed again—waiting for you to step inside.

With every step into the shadowed archway, the air thickened—heavy with stories untold and promises unkept. The spiral carved in stone seemed to pulse under your fingertips, alive with an energy both ancient and urgent.

She whispered, it's as if the labyrinth itself remembers us.

Armando's gaze swept the faded symbols lining the walls.

These markings... they're warnings, yes. But also invitations. To face not just the past, but ourselves.

The man from London tightened his grip on the pendant, his voice low but resolute.

If the face we saw once was a key, then this place is the lock. And what lies beyond will change everything.

The journal in your bag trembled lightly, pages fluttering open as if urging you forward.

You took a deep breath, stepping into the darkness beyond the archway.

The labyrinth wasn't just a place—it was a living puzzle, waiting for the next piece to fall into place.

And this time, you were ready to become that piece.

The darkness embraced you like an old secret, thick but not suffocating. Faint glimmers of light traced the spirals on the walls—guiding, teasing, beckoning.

She moved ahead with quiet confidence, her steps echoing softly.

Every turn is a question. Every shadow a choice.

Armando's voice broke the silence.

We're not chasing ghosts anymore. We're uncovering echoes—fragments of lives entwined with ours.

The man from London stopped, his eyes reflecting something deeper than fear—recognition.

This labyrinth... it's alive with their stories. Our stories.

You reached out, tracing the spiral once more. It felt warm now, like a heartbeat beneath stone.

A soft whisper rose from the depths—a voice both familiar and strange.

Find me where the light bends. Only then will the face reveal its truth.

The path ahead twisted, uncertain. But the promise lingered.

The walls seemed to breathe as you moved deeper, shadows stretching and folding like living things. The whisper repeated, growing clearer—

Find me where the light bends.

She paused beside a fractured mirror, shards catching stray beams and casting fractured rainbows across the corridor.

This must be it—the place where light refuses to stay straight.

Armando knelt, examining faint footprints etched in dust.

Someone was here recently... or maybe long ago, but their presence still lingers.

The man from London stepped forward, voice low and urgent.

If this is where the face will show itself, we must be ready—for truth, and for consequence.

You swallowed the rising tension and stepped closer to the mirror's fractured glow.

The spiral pulse quickened beneath your feet—heartbeats syncing with the rhythm of the labyrinth itself.

Then, in a sliver of reflected
light, the face appeared.

Not distant, not forgotten.

Alive. Watching. Waiting.

And the labyrinth whispered its final promise:

Welcome home.

The face held your gaze—familiar yet elusive, carved from shadows and light, a puzzle still unsolved.

She reached out tentatively, fingertips trembling as they brushed the fractured glass.

It's him... but not just him. It's all of us, intertwined in this maze of memory.

Armando's voice was steady, carrying the weight of revelation.

The man from London, the painter, the father—threads woven into the same tapestry.

The face flickered, shifting between past and present, pain and hope, loss and redemption.

You felt the labyrinth pulse stronger, as if breathing life into the story you thought was finished.

"This is the place where we rewrite the narrative," you said quietly, heart pounding.

The mirror cracked further, spilling light like promise breaking free.

Together, you stepped through—beyond mystery, beyond fear—into the truth waiting just ahead.

The journey wasn't over. It had only just begun.

Beyond the shattered mirror, a new world unfolded—fractured yet radiant, where memories and moments tangled in a delicate dance.

She looked around, eyes wide with wonder.

This isn't just a place. It's the crossroads of every choice we ever made.

Armando traced a path etched in glowing lines beneath the floor.

Each step here reshapes the past—and carves out the future.

The man from London tightened his grip on the pendant, voice steady.

We're no longer lost souls in a labyrinth. We're the architects of our own story.

You stepped forward, feeling the pulse of the spiral beneath your feet sync with your own heartbeat.

The face you saw once smiled—no longer a mystery, but a guide.

And as the light stretched around you, the labyrinth whispered:

Create your path. Break the cycle. Begin anew.

With courage, you took the next step—into the limitless unknown.

The air shimmered, thick with possibility. The walls around you dissolved into whispers of color and light, as if the labyrinth itself was unraveling to reveal what lay beyond.

She turned to you, eyes shining with a fierce certainty.

We've carried this weight too long—waiting for answers to find us. Now, we forge them ourselves.

Armando nodded, voice steady and sure.

The past can no longer chain us. We hold the key to freedom.

The man from London lifted the pendant, now glowing softly in his palm.

This isn't just about uncovering a face or a name. It's about reclaiming what was lost—identity, purpose, belonging.

You felt the journal warm against your side, its pages ready to capture every step of the journey ahead.

The spiral's pulse steadied—a heartbeat not of fear, but of hope.

Together, you stepped forward.

The labyrinth behind you faded, but the story—your story—had only just begun.

As you crossed the threshold, the world shifted—a landscape woven from fragments of memory and possibility. The air hummed with stories yet to be told, paths waiting to be chosen.

She reached into her pocket, pulling out a small, worn key—the one found hidden in the painter's forgotten sketchbook.

This unlocks more than doors, she said, voice low. It unlocks truth.

Armando studied the surroundings, tracing glowing symbols that seemed to respond to the key's presence.

Every labyrinth has its heart. This is ours.

The man from London stepped closer, eyes sharp.

If we're to find the answers—our answers—we must be ready to face what's buried in the deepest shadows.

You opened the journal again, and the pages wrote themselves:

In the labyrinth's heart, the past and future converge. Only those who dare to look beyond the mask find the way.

With the key in hand, you moved forward—toward the heart of the labyrinth, where the ultimate secret waited, silent and patient.

The figure's eyes met yours—holding both regret and a quiet resolve.

"My silence was a shield," he said softly. "From enemies who would tear us apart. From a world that didn't want the truth to surface."

She reached out, trembling, fingers brushing his hand.

"I carried your picture for years... never knowing if you were real or just a ghost."

He nodded, voice thick with emotion.

"Now, we have a chance to rewrite what was broken. To break the cycle."

Armando stepped forward, eyes scanning the chamber's walls—ancient symbols pulsing faintly.

"These markings... they speak of betrayal, of loss, but also of redemption. We're part of a story much bigger than ourselves."

You closed the journal, feeling the weight of the moment.

"This labyrinth wasn't just a prison. It was a test."

The man smiled faintly.

"And you passed."

Outside, the spiral outside hummed softly—a quiet promise of new beginnings.

Together, you faced the unknown.

No longer lost.

But chosen.

And ready.

The adventure wasn't just a search anymore.

It was a reckoning.

The deeper you ventured, the heavier the air became—thick with silence and anticipation. The labyrinth's heartbeat echoed in your chest, guiding you closer to its core.

She stopped before a massive door, etched with symbols that seemed to shift and rearrange beneath the key's touch.

This is it, she whispered. The threshold between what was hidden and what must be revealed.

Armando's voice was steady, almost reverent.

Beyond this door lies the truth we've been chasing—about the man, the painter, and the ties that bind us.

The man from London tightened his grip on the pendant, eyes never leaving the door.

No turning back now.

With a slow, deliberate motion, you slid the key into the lock. The mechanism hummed, ancient and alive, as the door began to open—revealing a chamber bathed in soft, golden light.

Inside, the air shimmered with memories—fragments of laughter, whispers, and forgotten promises.

At the center stood a figure, waiting—not quite a stranger, not quite a ghost.

The face you saw once.

The story's missing piece.

And the beginning of everything you never knew you needed to find.

The figure stepped forward, features shifting between clarity and shadow—like a half-remembered dream.

She gasped softly.

That's him... the man from the purse. My father?

He smiled, eyes heavy with stories untold.

I've waited long for you to find this place. For all of us to come together.

Armando's gaze hardened.

Why the silence? Why the disappearance.

The man's voice was steady but worn.

Because some truths are too dangerous to face until the time is right. But the labyrinth was never meant to hide me—it was meant to protect us.

The room pulsed with unspoken history, pain intertwined with hope.

You felt the journal's pages flutter, writing themselves anew:

The past is never lost. It waits, folded in shadows, ready to guide us forward.

Together, you stepped closer—toward answers, toward healing, and toward a future shaped by the choices you dared to make.

The labyrinth had opened its heart.

And so had you.

The figure's eyes met yours—holding both regret and a quiet resolve.

My silence was a shield, he said softly. From enemies who would tear us apart. From a world that didn't want the truth to surface.

She reached out, trembling, fingers brushing his hand.

I carried your picture for years... never knowing if you were real or just a ghost.

He nodded, voice thick with emotion.

Now, we have a chance to rewrite what was broken. To break the cycle.

Armando stepped forward, eyes scanning the chamber's walls—ancient symbols pulsing faintly.

These markings... they speak of betrayal, of loss, but also of redemption. We're part of a story much bigger than ourselves.

You closed the journal, feeling the weight of the moment.

This labyrinth wasn't just a prison. It was a test.

The man smiled faintly.

And you passed.

Outside, the spiral outside hummed softly—a quiet promise of new beginnings.

Together, you faced the unknown.

No longer lost.

But chosen.

And ready.

The chamber seemed to breathe around you, walls alive with whispered secrets and flickering shadows.

She looked to her father, eyes searching.

What now? How do we break free from this maze?

He took a deep breath, voice steady.

We begin by untangling the threads—one by one. The truth is a labyrinth itself, and only together can we navigate its twists.

Armando stepped forward, a determined glint in his eye.

We follow the signs left behind—the painter's strokes, the hidden messages in the portraits, the echoes of the past that still linger.

You opened the journal once more, its pages blank no longer, but a map of memories and possibilities.

This is our guide. Our way out—and our way forward.

The spiral outside pulsed brighter, a beacon in the dark.

With hands joined, you took the first step beyond the chamber.

The labyrinth was no longer a prison.

It was a passage.

A journey.

And the story was finally yours to write.

As you stepped beyond the chamber, the labyrinth's walls shifted again—this time revealing not walls, but open paths bathed in soft, golden light.

The air was thick with promise, but also a lingering tension, as if the maze itself was watching—waiting for your next move.

She glanced back at the fading door, then ahead at the unfolding paths.

This is where our choices begin. Each direction holds a secret, a challenge, a truth.

Armando studied the glowing symbols etched into the ground, then locked eyes with you.

We must be cautious. The labyrinth tests more than our courage—it tests our trust.

The man from London raised the pendant, its glow steady now, almost like a heartbeat syncing with yours.

"This journey isn't just about finding answers—it's about becoming the people we were meant to be."

You nodded, feeling the weight and wonder of it all.

The spiral pulsed beneath your feet once more—a reminder that every step forward was a step into the unknown, but also into possibility.

Together, you chose a path.

And the labyrinth—alive, watching, waiting—welcomed you.

The path ahead twisted unexpectedly, shadows weaving with light like a living

tapestry. Every step echoed with the hum of the labyrinth's unseen pulse.

She paused, fingers tracing the air as if following invisible threads.

There's more here than we imagined—layers beneath layers, secrets folded into riddles.

Armando's voice cut through the silence.

Each challenge will ask us to face what we fear most. But also, to remember who we truly are.

The man from London tightened his grip on the pendant, a flicker of doubt crossing his eyes.

And what if the labyrinth changes us? What if the person who emerges isn't the one who entered?

You swallowed hard but met their gaze.

Then we make sure we walk it together.

The walls around you shimmered, revealing faint glimpses of faces—past wanderers, lost hopes, silent watchers.

The spiral's heartbeat quickened, urging you onward.

Ahead, a fork in the path appeared—one veiled in darkness, the other glowing faintly with warm light.

The choice was yours.

And with it, the next step of the story waited—unwritten, infinite, alive.

You hesitated at the fork, feeling the weight of the choice press like a silent judge.

The dark path whispered of unknown fears, secrets buried deep—promises of truths that might unravel everything.

The glowing path beckoned with warmth, but also uncertainty—hope mingled with the risk of illusion.

She looked to you, eyes steady but vulnerable.

Which do you trust? The shadow of what was, or the light of what might be?

Armando stepped beside you, resolute.

Sometimes, the darkest paths lead to the brightest revelations.

The man from London nodded slowly, voice low.

We have no map for this. Only faith—in each other, and in the labyrinth's purpose.

You took a breath, heart pounding like the spiral beneath your feet.

Then, with quiet certainty, you stepped—

into the unknown.

Into the mystery.

Into the story only you could finish.

The shadows embraced you as you crossed the threshold, cool and heavy like a forgotten secret.

Whispers curled around your mind—half-voices, half-memories—pulling you deeper into the maze's hidden heart.

Shapes flickered at the edges of vision—faces you almost recognized, places you almost remembered.

She grasped your arm, steadying you.

This is where the labyrinth tests your soul. Where fear becomes the key.

Armando's voice was a steady anchor.

Trust the thread, even when it seems to fray.

The pendant pulsed softly, a steady heartbeat against the labyrinth's silence.

Ahead, a faint glow shimmered—an answer? A trap? No one could say.

But moving forward was the only way.

Step by step, breath by breath,

You walked deeper into the mystery—

toward the light buried in the dark.

With every step, the air grew thicker—heavy with memories both yours and those you never lived. The walls seemed to pulse, breathing in rhythm with your own heartbeat.

Suddenly, the faint glow ahead intensified, revealing a small alcove carved into the stone. Inside, a weathered chest rested, its surface etched with symbols matching those on the pendant.

She knelt beside it, tracing the carvings.

This chest... it's more than it seems. Like the labyrinth itself, it holds layers.

Armando's eyes narrowed.

Could this be the painter's secret? The key to the man's past?

The man from London hesitated, then pulled the pendant closer to the chest. The symbols shimmered, unlocking a soft click.

The lid creaked open, revealing a bundle of letters, faded photographs, and a small, intricately folded map—its edges worn by time and secrecy.

You reached in, fingers trembling.

Each piece felt like a fragment of a forgotten life... a puzzle waiting to be pieced together.

The labyrinth was no longer just a maze of stone and shadow.

It was a story—your story—waiting to be told.

You carefully unfolded the map, its lines twisting like the spiral beneath your feet, marking hidden paths and secret places long erased by time.

One photograph caught your eye—a man, eyes fierce but weary, standing beside a woman whose face was almost lost in shadow. A faint inscription on the back read: For those who seek the truth beyond the walls.

She whispered, this must be them—the painter and the father. Their story was hidden here all along.

Armando's voice was steady but urgent.

We follow the map. It leads to the heart of the labyrinth... and maybe to the answers we crave.

The man from London looked at you, determination hardening his gaze.

Whatever waits there, we face it together.

You folded the map carefully, the weight of history pressing on your shoulders. The spiral's pulse grew stronger, a rhythm that no longer felt threatening but guiding.

With a shared breath, you stepped forward—deeper into the maze, deeper into the past,

and closer to the truth that would change everything.

The corridors narrowed, walls closing in like the tightening grip of forgotten memories. The air was thick with dust and silence, broken only by the faint echo of your footsteps.

The map led you to a heavy iron door, its surface scarred but bearing the same spiral symbol that had haunted your journey.

She reached out, fingertips grazing the cold metal.

This is it—the heart.

Armando pressed a hidden latch revealed by the map's clues. The door groaned open, revealing a chamber bathed in dim, flickering light.

Inside, a canvas stretched across the far wall—unfinished, but alive with color and shadow. The painter's final work, a labyrinth within a labyrinth, capturing the chaos and beauty of the maze itself.

At its center, the man from the photo stood tall, face unreadable—but behind him, the faintest outline of a woman—her eyes locked with yours.

You realized then—the story wasn't just about the past.

It was about the choices still waiting to be made.

And the mysteries still yearning to be uncovered.

The labyrinth was no longer a prison.

It was an invitation.

To walk the spiral,

and become the story.

You stepped closer to the canvas, feeling a strange pull—as if the painted figures were reaching out, inviting you inside their world.

She whispered, the painter vanished, but his spirit lingers here, in this unfinished work.

Armando traced the spiral in the painting with his finger, and suddenly, the room shifted—the walls melting away to reveal a new passage carved behind the canvas.

The man from London turned to you, eyes fierce with resolve.

This is the next step. Whatever lies beyond, it holds the final truth.

With a steady breath, you crossed the threshold into darkness, guided only by the spiral's pulse.

Ahead, whispers grew louder—stories waiting to be told, secrets aching to be freed.

And you understood: the labyrinth was more than stone and shadow—it was the map of your soul, winding ever deeper, toward a destiny only you could choose.

The passage swallowed you whole, cool and silent, the spiral's pulse now a steady drum in your chest. Shadows flickered like memories—some welcoming, others warning.

She stopped, fingers brushing a carved inscription on the wall, half-hidden by time:

To face the past is to unlock the future.

Armando's voice broke the silence.

We're close. The answers, the man from London's past, your friend's father—they're all threads in the same weave.

The air shifted—thick with anticipation, with the weight of all that had been lost and all that could still be found.

Ahead, a faint light glimmered—a door, or perhaps a revelation.

You stepped forward, heart steady, ready to unravel the final knot of the labyrinth.

Because sometimes, the greatest mysteries aren't in what's hidden—but in the courage to uncover them.

The light grew stronger as you approached, casting long shadows that danced on the walls like restless spirits. The door before you were unlike any other—carved from dark wood veined with silver, etched with symbols both ancient and unfamiliar.

She placed her hand on the door, hesitating. This is where the past and future meet.

Armando tightened his grip on your shoulder. No turning back now.

With a shared nod, you pushed the door open.

Inside was a small chamber, its walls lined with letters, journals, and sketches—fragments of a life shrouded in mystery. At the center, a weathered wooden box rested on a pedestal.

You reached out, fingers trembling, and lifted the lid.

Inside lay a single object—a locket, worn and delicate, but unmistakably hers.

The labyrinth had led you here, to the truth buried beneath layers of silence.

And as the spiral pulse faded, a new rhythm began—one of discovery, healing, and the promise of what was yet to come.

You held the locket gently, feeling its weight — more than metal, it carried years of secrets and untold stories. The clasp creaked open, revealing a faded photograph inside: a woman's face, serene yet hauntingly familiar.

She breathed softly, This... this is her. My mother.

Armando's eyes darkened. And the man we've been chasing — your father — must be connected to all of this.

A sudden draft whispered through the chamber, stirring the scattered papers. One journal slid forward, opening to a page filled with a map and a cryptic note: Find the spiral's end — where shadows meet light.

The labyrinth wasn't finished with you yet.

With the locket in your palm and the map in your hands, you knew the next path awaited — deeper into mystery, closer to the heart of truth.

And this time, the journey was as much about what you would discover inside yourself as in the labyrinth's winding corridors.

You traced the faded ink on the journal's map, the lines twisting like the spiral that had guided you so far. The note echoed in your mind—where shadows meet light.

She looked at you, eyes wide but steady.

This is more than a place. It's a moment, a crossing point.

Armando nodded, voice low and certain.

Whatever lies at the spiral's end will change everything. It's not just about the past anymore—it's about what we choose to become.

The chamber seemed to breathe around you, the walls pulsing with anticipation.

Together, you stepped back into the labyrinth's embrace—ready to follow the map's final thread, to face the shadows, and to step into the light waiting beyond.

The story wasn't over. It was just unfolding.

The labyrinth twisted ahead, the air thick with a mix of anticipation and unease. Every step echoed with the weight of the past and the promise of revelation.

The map led you down a narrow stairwell, carved into ancient stone, spiraling deeper than you had imagined. The walls here were etched with symbols—some matching the spiral, others foreign, yet strangely familiar.

At the bottom, a cavern opened before you, lit by a shaft of light streaming from an unseen source above. In the center stood a pedestal, blank but for a single inscription:

Here, the shadow meets the light. Here, the story becomes whole.

She stepped forward, her voice barely a whisper.

This is it. The end of the spiral.

Armando glanced at you, determination burning in his eyes.

Are you ready?

With a steady breath, you nodded. Together, you reached toward the pedestal — the moment of truth finally within reach.

Your fingers brushed the pedestal's surface, cool and smooth, and the light shifted—warping, bending like a veil lifting.

Suddenly, the chamber dissolved around you.

You found yourself standing not in stone, but in memory—vivid, alive. A room filled with laughter, arguments, love, and loss. Faces blurred and sharp, moments tangled across time.

There, at the center, was the man—the father—watching you with eyes full of regrets and untold stories.

She gasped,

tears tracing down her cheeks.

So much was hidden... but it all led here.

Armando's voice was steady, even in this fragile space.

The labyrinth was never meant to trap you. It was meant to guide you home.

You reached out, bridging past and present, knowing the true journey had only just begun.

The memories swirled around you, each one a fragment of truth waiting to be embraced. The man's gaze softened, and in that moment, the weight of years seemed to lift between you.

She stepped forward, voice trembling but resolute.

Why did you leave? Why hide from me?

His eyes held a quiet sorrow.

I was lost in shadows, tangled in debts and dangers I thought I could protect you from. I never wanted you to carry my darkness.

You watched as the scene shifted—a flash of the man in London, the portrait, the hidden tunnels, the spiral—all threads weaving into a tapestry of sacrifice and survival.

Armando placed a hand
on your shoulder.

The labyrinth tested you, but it also revealed the strength you carry inside.

The light around you brightened, the past and present merging.

You realized then: the true labyrinth was never the tunnels or the spirals. It was the journey within—the courage to face what's hidden, to forgive, and to choose your own path forward.

And as the memory faded, you stepped back into the chamber, ready to write the next chapter—one of truth, healing, and new beginnings.

Back in the chamber, the locket still warm in your hand, a quiet resolve settled over you. The labyrinth's pulse slowed, now steady like a heartbeat you could trust.

She looked at you, eyes shining with a mixture of grief and hope.

This changes everything. My past, my future—it's all clearer now.

Armando gave a rare, small smile.

We've uncovered the shadows. Now it's time to build the light.

Together, you gathered the journals, the map, the fragments of stories—each one a piece of the puzzle that was no longer just mystery, but inheritance.

Outside, the spiral glowed softly in the dawn light, no longer a trap but a promise.

And as you stepped out of the labyrinth, you knew this was only the beginning. The face you saw once had become the path you chose to follow—toward truth, toward freedom, and toward whatever lay beyond the next turn.

The city outside stirred awake, Prague's cobblestones glistening with morning dew, but inside you carried a quiet revolution.

The labyrinth had peeled back layers—not just of stone and shadow, but of identity, legacy, and choice.

She slipped the locket around her neck, a symbol now not just of mystery, but of belonging.

Armando pulled a worn notebook from his coat. There's more out there. Threads we haven't touched, secrets still waiting.

You felt the weight of the journey ahead but also the thrill of possibility.

The spiral never ends, you said, voice steady. It only leads us forward.

And with that, the three of you stepped into the unfolding day—ready to chase the next mystery, uncover the next truth, and live the story that was yours to write.

As you walked away from the labyrinth's entrance, the city's hum wrapped around you like a second skin—alive unpredictable, full of whispers waiting to be heard.

The locket swung gently at her chest, a heartbeat tethered to the past yet guiding her forward. The journal's pages rustled in Armando's hand, promising new riddles and deeper truths.

You glanced back once, catching the fading glow of the spiral etched into the stone. It wasn't an end but a beginning—an invitation to keep unraveling the layers, to dive into shadows and light alike.

Where to next? she asked, eyes bright with newfound purpose.

You smiled, the weight of uncertainty now a spark for adventure.

Anywhere the labyrinth leads us. Because every path hides a story—and we're here to find them all.

And with that, you stepped into the unfolding mystery, the story continuing—one breath, one choice, one step at a time.

The streets narrowed, winding like the threads of the labyrinth itself, pulling you deeper into the city's hidden veins.

A whisper in the wind—an old song, a warning, or maybe an invitation.

Armando's eyes scanned the shadows, every corner a promise or a threat.

She clutched the locket tighter, feeling its warmth pulse in time with her heartbeat.

Ahead, a narrow alley glimmered faintly, walls adorned with faded graffiti—symbols matching those in the labyrinth.

This is no coincidence, you said, stepping forward.

With every step, the past and present tangled, and the next secret waited to be uncovered.

The labyrinth was far from over. It was only deepening.

The alley breathed secrets its shadows stretching like fingers inviting you in.

You hesitated, then stepped forward, the symbols on the walls glowing faintly beneath your touch.

A hidden door appeared, almost seamless with the brick—a threshold between worlds.

She looked at you, eyes steady.

This is it. The next step.

Armando drew a deep breath, ready to follow whatever lay beyond.

Together, you crossed the threshold, the air shifting as the labyrinth unfolded anew.

And somewhere in the darkness ahead, the next truth waited—patient, elusive, alive.

To be continued...

Inside, the air was thick with silence — a heavy, expectant quiet that seemed to press against your skin.

The walls pulsed softly, the symbols now glowing brighter, guiding your way deeper into the unknown.

Footsteps echoed, but they weren't just yours. Somewhere ahead, a shadow moved — deliberate, watching, waiting.

She tightened her grip on the locket, sensing the weight of history pressing close.

Armando whispered, We're not alone.

Heart pounding, you took the lead, each step drawing you closer to a secret that refused to stay buried.

The labyrinth was waking — and so were the shadows within.

The passage twisted sharply, narrowing as it descended into darkness. The faint glow of the symbols flickered like distant stars, casting long shadows that danced on the walls.

Suddenly, a soft voice whispered—barely audible, but unmistakably human.

"Why do you seek what should remain hidden?"

You froze. The air grew colder, heavier.

She swallowed, stepping closer to you.

"We seek truth. Not to destroy, but to understand."

A figure emerged from the shadows — neither fully friend nor foe. His eyes held centuries of secrets, pain, and something fragile: hope.

You walk the labyrinth willingly, he said, voice low. Few do. But beware—the deeper you go, the more you become part of the maze.

Armando tightened his grip on the notebook.

Then we walk carefully... but we do not turn back.

The maze had spoken. The journey was far from over.

The stranger stepped forward, the dim light revealing a weathered face marked by time and burden.

"My name is Elias," he said. "Keeper of paths long forgotten. You seek answers, but beware—some truths demand a price."

She looked at him, steady.

"I've paid more than enough already."

Elias nodded slowly.

"Then follow me. The labyrinth isn't just walls and shadows—it's memory, blood, and choice. What you uncover may change everything you thought you knew."

The three of you moved deeper, the air thick with anticipation. The spiral wasn't just a symbol anymore—it was a warning and a guide.

And somewhere beyond the next turn, the heart of the labyrinth awaited—where past, present, and future collided in a single breath.

The corridor opened into a vast chamber, walls adorned with faded frescoes—stories of forgotten lives, lost loves, and silent betrayals.

In the center, an ancient stone pedestal held a weathered book, its cover etched with the same spiral that had haunted your journey.

Elias gestured toward it.

This is the Codex of Echoes—the labyrinth's memory.

Every secret, every choice ever made here, recorded in its pages.

She hesitated, fingers trembling as she reached out.

Is this what we've been searching for?

Elias's eyes held a warning.

Not just what you've been searching for. But what you must face.

As the book opened, the chamber seemed to breathe, the walls whispering echoes of the past, and the labyrinth's true story began to unfold.

The air grew heavier, shadows thickening as the chamber's whispers turned darker—echoes of fear, terror, and death long buried beneath the labyrinth's stone bones.

Each step forward felt like crossing a thin line between hope and ruin.

Elias's voice dropped to a grave tone:

The labyrinth feeds on fear—on the sacrifices made to keep its secrets hidden. To face it is to risk everything.

She swallowed hard, clutching the locket like a lifeline.

We don't have a clear future. Only the choice to fight for one.

The Codex's pages turned on their own, revealing names, faces, lives lost—and the faintest glimmers of salvation buried within the darkness.

You realized then: the labyrinth wasn't just a place. It was a living testament to human resilience—the tangled dance of terror and hope, sacrifice and survival.

And the path forward. Unknown.

But you would walk it anyway.

The chamber's walls seemed to close in, the whispers now rising into a chorus of desperate voices—echoes of those who had vanished within the labyrinth's grasp.

Elias pointed to a faded inscription carved beneath the frescoes:

To unravel the maze, one must face the shadow within.

She met your eyes, determination flickering through the fear.

Then we face it together.

The Codex pulsed faintly, revealing a hidden passage—narrow, twisting, and swallowed by darkness.

With every step, the weight of the past pressed heavier, but so did the promise of a future unbound by fear.

The labyrinth's heart awaited. And inside it, the truth that could either destroy you—or set you free.

You took a breath.

And stepped forward.

The passage narrowed, cold stone pressing close on all sides, as if the labyrinth itself was holding its breath.

Your footsteps echoed, swallowed quickly by the thick silence.

A sudden flicker of movement—a shadow darted at the edge of your vision, vanishing before you could react.

She gripped your arm, whispering, We're not alone down here.

Elias's voice came low, steady:

The labyrinth tests not just your courage, but your truth. Every fear, every doubt—it will bring them to light.

Ahead, faint light spilled from a chamber door, worn and ancient.

Beyond it, you sensed the final thread—fragile, dangerous, and calling you deeper into the maze's secret heart.

Together, you pushed open the door.

And the air changed.

The truth waited.

Inside, the chamber breathed with a heavy silence, thick with the weight of untold stories.

Walls covered in cryptic symbols pulsed faintly, alive like the heartbeat of the labyrinth itself.

In the center, a mirror — cracked and dusted with time — stood framed by twisted iron.

She stepped forward, eyes locked on her reflection — but the face staring back was not quite her own.

A voice, barely more than a breath, whispered from the shadows:

Who are you when the masks fall away.

You felt the labyrinth's true challenge begin — not a fight with monsters, but a reckoning with the self.

The path forward was no longer a mystery of walls and tunnels.

It was the courage to face the unknown within.

And to decide what kind of story you would write next.

Her reflection shimmered, flickering between who she was and who she feared to become.

The cracked mirror seemed less a barrier and more a portal—one that demanded she confront every hidden fragment of her past.

You carry more than secrets," the voice murmured, "you carry the weight of choices undone.

You stepped closer, heart pounding.

This isn't just about the labyrinth anymore. It's about breaking the cycle.

She nodded slowly, tears glistening but unyielding.

To find light, I must first walk through darkness.

Behind you, the labyrinth whispered — no longer a prison, but a guide.

And in that silence, a new resolve took shape: to rewrite the story, not as victims of fear, but as authors of their own fate.

The mirror cracked further, and the path ahead opened — uncertain, yes, but truly free.

As the mirror fractured, shards of reflection scattered like fractured memories, each revealing glimpses of forgotten moments—laughter lost, promises broken, and hope nearly buried.

She reached out, fingertips grazing the sharp edges, embracing the pain woven into her history.

You're ready, the voice said, softer now, almost gentle.

Elias stepped forward, holding a small, ancient key.

This opens the final door — the one between what was, what is, and what could be.

Together, you moved toward a hidden archway that appeared behind the mirror's glow, a threshold shimmering with possibility.

With a breath, she took the key and turned it.

The door swung open, revealing not darkness — but a horizon bathed in dawn's first light.

In that moment, the labyrinth released its hold, and the story truly began.

Stepping through the threshold, the weight of the labyrinth began to lift, replaced by a quiet clarity.

The dawn spilled like liquid gold, warming the skin and filling the chest with a breath long held.

She looked at you, eyes shining—not with certainty, but with readiness to face whatever came next.

The maze was never about finding an exit, she said softly, it was about finding myself.

Beyond the light, new paths stretched—unwritten, unpredictable, and alive with possibility.

You realized then that every step forward was a choice: to embrace fear, or to create hope.

And as the sun climbed higher, the labyrinth's spiral became not a cage, but a symbol—a beginning, not an end.

The journey had changed.

And so, had you.

The story was far from over.

But even as the light warmed your faces, a faint shadow lingered at the edge of vision—

a reminder that every journey carries its own unseen dangers.

The labyrinth's mysteries had not fully surrendered, only shifted into new forms.

You both knew the past was never truly left behind.

It followed, whispered in forgotten places, waiting for the next step, the next choice.

Yet now, armed with truth and courage, the unknown no longer held the power to paralyze.

Instead, it beckoned—an invitation to keep moving, keep uncovering, keep becoming.

And so, hand in hand, you stepped forward—into the mystery, into the light, and into the next chapter of the story.

As you moved forward, the horizon stretched wide—an endless maze of possibilities waiting to be explored.

Each step echoed with the weight of history but also the promise of transformation.

The face once seen in a fleeting moment now carried the power to unlock not just doors, but destinies.

Your journey was no longer just about uncovering secrets buried in shadow—it was about weaving them into something new, something whole.

The labyrinth had taught you that mystery and truth are intertwined, and that sometimes, the greatest courage is to keep walking, even when the path is unknown.

With every breath, you embraced the unfolding story—one not bound by fear, but alive with hope.

And somewhere, deep within the spiral, a new light began to glow—waiting for the next step, the next revelation, the next beginning.

The glow grew stronger, pulsing like a heartbeat beneath the surface of the world.

It was a call—not just to you, but to all who dared to seek beyond the walls of certainty.

In that light, past and future intertwined, revealing threads that connected forgotten faces, lost moments, and hidden truths.

Your friend's search for her father, the painter's vanished legacy, the man in the photograph—all were part of a tapestry larger than any of you had imagined.

The labyrinth was not just a place, but a living story, forever shifting, always waiting for new hands to trace its spirals.

As the sun rose higher, you felt it—

the invitation to step deeper, to risk more, to embrace the mystery without fear.

And with that, the journey continued.

Because some stories never truly end—they only evolve, as long as there are hearts brave enough to follow the spiral.

The glow pulsed stronger now, guiding you deeper into the labyrinth's heart.

Around you, the air thickened with whispers—half-heard voices threading through the stone corridors like ghosts of forgotten truths.

Your friend's eyes never left the photograph, her breath steady but tense.

I think he's here, she said, voice barely more than a breath.

A sudden draft stirred the shadows, and the walls seemed to shift, revealing a narrow passage carved with symbols—ancient, cryptic, and alive with meaning.

With every step, the weight of the past pressed heavier, but so did the pull of the promise—the chance to finally uncover what was lost.

You reached out, tracing the symbols, feeling their energy ripple through your fingertips.

The labyrinth wasn't just a place of fear.

It was a place of awakening.

And the face in the photograph was no longer just a mystery—it was the key.

The key—yes, but not in the way you first imagined.

It wasn't about unlocking a door.

It was about unlocking memory. Blood. Identity.

The symbols beneath your hand warmed, glowing faintly as though responding to the presence of the photograph now held between you both.

The narrow corridor began to breathe with a strange rhythm—as if the labyrinth itself recognized her.

Your friend stepped forward, holding the photo up like a relic.

And then, from the stone—

a soft click.

A hidden panel shifted, revealing an alcove carved into the wall. Inside: a single object.

A portrait.

Aged, dust-covered, but unmistakable.

The same man. The same face.

Painted in the style of a forgotten era, with a signature in the corner neither of you recognized—but one she whispered aloud:

....my mother spoke of this name. The painter who vanished.

Beneath the canvas, folded carefully, lay a letter. Unopened. Sealed with wax.

Her hands trembled.

And somewhere behind you, the labyrinth shifted again.

As if something else had awakened.

She broke the seal. Slowly. Carefully.

Inside, the letter was yellowed but intact, the handwriting sharp, deliberate—like someone had written it knowing it might be read decades later.

To the daughter I could never hold—

If you've found this, then the spiral has brought you home.

I was never lost. I was hidden. For your protection. For hers.

But truth will not sleep forever.

You are the thread now.

She looked up at you, eyes wide—not with fear, but with something deeper. Recognition. Inheritance.

Beneath the letter was a second photo—blurry, but recent. The same man. Alive. Older.

Stamped with the name of a town. Eastern border. Forest. Mountains.

A place neither of you had ever heard of.

The labyrinth had done its part.

Now the real path was calling. Beyond the tunnels. Beyond myth.

Not to chase ghosts—

but to find the living.

She folded the letter with reverence, as if sealing a vow within her chest.

The portrait, the name, the town—they weren't just fragments anymore. They were coordinates. A map drawn in memory and silence.

You stepped out of the alcove, and the labyrinth behind you began to dim, its walls softening into shadow, like a dream retreating at dawn. It had given all it could.

Outside, the air was colder. Sharper. More real.

And in that crisp silence, something shifted inside both of you.

No longer just wanderers.

Now seekers.

She tucked the photo beside her heart.

We leave at first light, she said.

You nodded, though you both knew—

light wasn't something you waited for

anymore.

It was something you carried.

The road stretched out before you—uncharted, silent, yet vibrating with the weight of what lay ahead.

Not just geography.

History. Legacy. Blood.

The town mentioned in the photo was remote, almost erased from modern maps. But that made sense now. Whoever had

hidden the man had done so with care, and for a reason.

As dawn broke, your train carved through

a landscape both foreign and oddly familiar—thick forests, fog-laced hills, and villages that seemed paused in time.

Your friend stared out the window, her fingers lightly brushing the sealed letter again and again. Not to read it—she'd memorized every word. But to remind herself it was real.

This place, she murmured, it's not just where he is. It's where she ended.

You didn't need to ask who. Her mother's silence had always been the loudest inheritance.

When the train slowed near a nameless stop—just a weathered sign and a dirt path—you both stood.

No crowd. No sound. Just wind and waiting.

The labyrinth may have been left behind.

But the spiral had only just begun to widen.

The dirt path led through pine and shadow, the air thick with damp moss and the scent of something older than memory. Every step forward felt like walking deeper into a story that hadn't finished being written.

The village emerged slowly—stone houses huddled close like secrets, shutters closed despite the rising sun. It wasn't abandoned. Just... watching.

An old woman sweeping outside a chapel paused mid-motion as you passed. Her eyes narrowed, then widened slightly—not in fear, but in recognition. She muttered something under her breath. A name.

Your friend turned.

Did she say Elias.

You both stopped.

The old woman nodded once, slowly. Then pointed—upward, toward the tree line where a single cabin clung to the slope like it had refused to fall.

There was no need to speak.

You both knew: he was there.

As you climbed the hill, the wind rose—carrying faint traces of ash, cedar, and something else... oil paint.

A life unfinished.

At the door, your friend hesitated. Her hand trembled as she reached up to knock—

but before she could, it opened from the inside.

And the face that met hers—older, worn, deeply human—

was the same one from the photograph.

Only now, the eyes weren't frozen in time.

They were full of it.

Neither of them spoke.

Not at first.

She stared—like trying to match two layers of memory that had never quite lined up. He stood in the doorway, silent, as if the years had taught him that some reunions demand stillness before sound.

Then:

"...you look like her."

His voice cracked like old wood.

Your friend swallowed hard. "She kept your picture. Hidden. All her life."

He stepped back, slowly, and motioned you both inside.

The cabin was sparse but strangely luminous. Paintings leaned against every surface — half-finished portraits, landscapes that blurred into dreams, and one... covered in a white sheet.

You were supposed to never find me, he said. But I left the thread anyway. In case the spiral turned again.

She glanced at the covered canvas.

What's under that?

He hesitated. I started it before she left. I couldn't finish it... until now.

She stepped closer.

And pulled the cloth away.

It was her. Not as a child. Not as a memory. But as she stood now — seen, known, even before they'd met.

I painted what I hoped you'd become, he said. Not knowing if I ever would.

And suddenly, time bent.

Not to erase the past — but to make room for the healing of it.

Tears didn't fall right away. They hung between them—like the words unsaid, the letters never written, the years lost to silence.

She reached out and touched the edge of the canvas.

Her voice came soft, but steady.

You saw me... even when I didn't know who I was.

He nodded once. That's what a father should do. Even from a distance.

The fire crackled behind you, and for a long while, no one moved.

Then he opened a drawer beneath the table and pulled out a small, weathered notebook. The same symbol etched faintly on the cover: the spiral.

I kept track, he said. Of dreams. Of names. Of the places I painted that never existed... but always led back to you.

She took it in both hands, breath catching.

There, on the first page:

A map not of land, but of longing.

You looked between them—two people once separated by silence, now stitched together by a thread stronger than blood: recognition.

The labyrinth hadn't been a trap.

It had been the only way through.

Outside, snow began to fall softly.

And inside, a beginning finally arrived.

She sat beside him now, no longer needing answers—only presence.

There was a warmth in the room that had nothing to do with the fire. It came from the stillness between them, the unspoken forgiveness, and the fragile peace that follows long storms.

He opened the notebook again, flipping to a page marked with a red thread. A sketch: the labyrinth, yes—but not the one of myth. This was something else. Shifting. Alive.

A place I dreamed often, he said. Where people walked into memory, but left with purpose.

He looked at her. I think you've been walking it longer than you know.

She traced the spiral on the page. And now?

He smiled faintly. Now... we find the door.

You leaned in. What door.

He stood slowly and walked to a cabinet built into the wall. Unlocking it, he pulled out a worn wooden box. Inside: a key. Old, iron-forged, its bow shaped like an open eye.

I painted it into every canvas, waiting for someone who could see it.

He handed it to her. There's a chapel in the woods. Abandoned. Except it isn't. Beneath it... the final layer.

She held the key, eyes wide. Not with fear.

With recognition.

Because some doors don't open to the unknown—

they open from it.

She turned the key over in her hands. It felt heavier than iron—like it carried echoes.

He watched her closely. I never went back. I couldn't. But you... you might be the one who's supposed to.

You looked to her, and she met your gaze. No words needed—only the silent nod between travelers who know the path won't wait forever.

At dawn, you set out.

The snow had deepened, but the trees cleared for your steps. Each branch bowed slightly as if guiding you. Birds were silent. The world had tucked itself into reverence.

And then, there it was.

The chapel. Small. Weatherworn. Ivy clung to its bones like memory refusing to die.

Inside, the air was warmer than it should've been.

A narrow aisle. Cracked pews. At the front: an altar—
and behind it, a painting.

Faded. Torn. But unmistakable.

The labyrinth.

Not just drawn, but layered—stitched with thread, ash, gold leaf.
At its center, something glimmered faintly: a small, hidden keyhole.

She stepped forward.

Her hand didn't tremble this time.

The key slid in as if it had always waited.

A click. A shift. The painting rippled—then pulled back, revealing
a passage. Not stone. Not shadow.

Light.

Pulsing, living, ancient.

She turned to you, eyes wide. It's not an ending.

No, you whispered. It's the real beginning.

And together, you stepped through.

The light didn't blind—it revealed.

As you stepped through the opening, the passage expanded, not
downward like a tunnel, but outward like a memory being
remembered. Walls shimmered, shifting between stone, canvas, and
sky.

Here, the labyrinth wasn't a prison.

It was a library.

Each corridor a chapter. Each door a decision never taken.

She paused before one: an old wooden archway covered in
symbols—some ancient, some impossibly new. Her fingers brushed the
frame.

A voice echoed faintly—not aloud, but within.

Her mother's.

....you were never lost. Just hidden.

Inside the room: a portrait. Unfinished. The lines faint but
unmistakable. The same man. Her father.

But beside him—another face. Hers.

Only younger. Watching him paint.

Tears welled. He knew me...

You stepped closer, and saw what she saw now:

The labyrinth wasn't just walked.

It was painted, memory by memory.

And some memories refused to fade.

In the center of the room was a pedestal. Upon it, a book.

Blank. Waiting.

She looked at you. What if the rest... is up to us?

You smiled. Then let's not just tell the story.

Let's live it.

She picked up the brush. And the labyrinth, once feared, opened not into terror—

—but into freedom.

The brush felt alive in her hand, like it was connected to something far deeper than paint or canvas.

Each stroke traced a memory, a possibility, a thread weaving the past with the future.

The walls around you seemed to breathe with the rhythm of her painting, colors swirling, forming shapes—faces,

places, moments never lived but somehow known.

You realized the labyrinth was no longer just a maze—it was a map.

A map of lost stories, hidden truths, and the fragile hope of redemption.

As she painted, the portrait of the man—the father—began to shift. His eyes met hers, clear and steady.

You're not alone, the image seemed to say.

Outside, the air shifted. The labyrinth pulsed softer now, like a heart slowing to rest.

You both understood. This was not the end.

It was a beginning rewritten—by choice, by courage, by love.

And somewhere deep inside, a door you never saw before was quietly unlocking.

Because sometimes, the most profound journeys start when you paint your own path.

The labyrinth waits—but now, so do you.

The door before you creaked open, revealing a narrow stairway spiraling down into darkness.

Your heart quickened—not with fear, but anticipation.

Each step echoed with whispers—fragments of forgotten conversations, lost hopes, warnings never heeded.

At the bottom, a chamber stretched wide, its walls lined with aged manuscripts and faded maps.

In the center, a solitary figure sat hunched over a desk—a man cloaked in shadow, his face obscured.

He looked up slowly. His eyes held storms of secrets, pain, and something else—recognition.

You've come, he said, voice rough but steady.

She stepped forward, clutching the brush tighter. Who are you?

The man's gaze softened. The keeper of the labyrinth's truth. And perhaps... the key to your past.

He slid a folded letter across the desk.

She unfolded it with trembling hands.

The handwriting was hers—only older, wiser.

To the daughter I never met, the truth you seek lies not in shadows, but in the courage to face them.

The labyrinth wasn't just a maze of stone—it was a maze of choice.

And now, the real journey had begun.

She swallowed hard, eyes fixed on the letter as the man rose slowly from his chair.

I was once like you, he said, voice heavy with regret. Searching for answers in places meant to stay hidden.

He stepped closer, the dim light revealing scars that mapped his history—both physical and unseen.

The labyrinth tests more than your steps. It tests your soul.

You felt the weight of those words settling between you like a heavy fog.

But, he continued, it also offers a choice: to remain lost, or to find your way forward.

She folded the letter carefully. Why show yourself now?

He smiled faintly, Because the past has a way of catching up... and sometimes, the only way out is through.

A distant rumble shook the chamber.

The labyrinth was shifting again—its secrets stirring, ready to be uncovered.

You exchanged a glance—equal parts fear and determination.

Together, you stepped deeper into the unknown.

Because some mysteries are meant to be lived, not just solved.

The air grew thick with a scent of damp earth and forgotten time as you ventured further into the labyrinth's depths.

The walls now seemed to pulse with faint, ghostly light—like the heartbeat of the maze itself.

The man led the way, his steps steady but cautious.

You must understand, he said, this labyrinth is not merely stone and shadow. It holds memories—both yours and mine, intertwined.

She reached out, brushing her fingers against the cool wall. Suddenly, an image flickered—her mother's face, fading into the face of the man from the portrait.

A whisper floated through the chamber:

Remember who you are.

Questions swirled, tangled like the paths beneath your feet.

Who was this man truly?

What was the secret her mother kept so fiercely.

And why was the labyrinth calling her back, again and again.

Ahead, a faint glow beckoned—an exit, or perhaps another beginning.

With resolve, you both moved forward, stepping into the light and the unknown.

Because sometimes, the only way out of a labyrinth... is through its heart.

The glow grew warmer, revealing an ancient archway etched with symbols that seemed both foreign and hauntingly familiar.

She reached out, tracing the carvings with trembling fingers.

The language of the labyrinth, the man whispered, a code passed down through generations.

Suddenly, the

ground beneath shifted, and the walls began to hum—a deep, resonant sound vibrating through your bones.

From the shadows, a figure emerged—a woman cloaked in white, her eyes sharp and knowing.

You seek answers, she said, voice like wind through leaves. But answers come with a price.

The man stepped protectively forward. She must decide.

The woman's gaze locked with hers, piercing and gentle.

Will you face the truth, no matter where it leads? Or will you turn back to the safety of shadows.

Silence stretched, thick as the labyrinth's walls.

She inhaled deeply, heart steady now.

I will walk the path, wherever it takes me.

The woman nodded, a faint smile breaking through the mystery.

Then step forward, and let the labyrinth reveal its final secret.

The archway glowed brighter, opening onto a passage bathed in golden light.

You stepped through—into the unknown, but no longer afraid.

The passage ahead pulsed with warmth, each step forward unraveling the threads of the past and weaving new ones into the future.

The air shimmered as scenes unfolded—visions of forgotten faces, whispered promises, and choices long buried beneath layers of time.

She saw her mother's laughter, fragile and fleeting, then the stern eyes of the man in the portrait, watching over a secret too heavy to carry alone.

The woman in white moved beside her, a silent guide through memory and meaning.

Suddenly, the path split—two doors, each marked with a symbol:

One bore the spiral, the eternal journey of seeking and becoming.

The other, a key—unlocking truth, but at a cost unknown.

Her hand hovered, torn between the pull of discovery and the weight of consequence.

The man's voice broke the silence, steady but grave:

Every choice shapes the labyrinth. Choose wisely—for some doors, once opened, never close.

She took a breath, heart steady, and reached for...

Her fingers brushed the door marked with the spiral—the symbol of endless journeys and transformations.

The moment her touch met the cool surface, the labyrinth sighed, as if waking from a long slumber.

The door swung open, revealing a chamber filled with shifting shadows and flickering lights—images that danced like memories refusing to be forgotten.

She stepped inside, the air thick with voices—whispers of those lost and found, love and betrayal, courage and fear.

The woman in white stayed at the threshold, watching silently.

Ahead, a figure emerged from the darkness—the man from the portrait, but younger, vibrant, and alive.

His eyes locked with hers, full of questions and untold stories.

You've come, he said softly. But are you ready to see what lies beneath the surface?

She swallowed hard, knowing the labyrinth was no longer just a place—it was a mirror reflecting everything she feared and hoped to find.

With a steady breath, she nodded.

Show me.

The shadows parted, revealing a path deeper into the heart of the mystery—where truth awaited, and the past was never truly gone.

The path ahead twisted like a serpent, walls closing in with whispers that echoed from forgotten corners of time.

Every step pulled her deeper into a mosaic of memories — fractured, raw, and aching with unanswered questions.

The man from the portrait led silently, his presence both a comfort and a challenge.

As they moved forward, the shadows coalesced into scenes: a hidden meeting in a rain-soaked alley, a desperate letter never sent, a hand slipping away in the dark.

Each vision chipped away at the veil between past and present.

Then, suddenly, the labyrinth trembled.

A low rumble, as if the earth itself was warning them — a choice was coming, and with it, the risk of losing everything.

She turned to him, eyes fierce.

I've come this far. No turning back.

He nodded, voice barely a whisper:

Then prepare. The truth is never as simple as it seems.

The corridor ahead split again — light on one side, darkness on the other.

With resolve, she stepped toward the unknown.

She chose the path shrouded in darkness, drawn by the promise of truths hidden beneath the surface.

The air grew colder, the silence heavier, broken only by the faint drip of water echoing through the tunnels.

Every step felt like walking deeper into a dream — or a nightmare — where memories blurred and shadows whispered secrets not meant to be heard.

Ahead, a door appeared, carved with the same spiral from the beginning but now cracked, as if the labyrinth itself was fracturing.

The man reached out, placing a steady hand on her shoulder.

This is where the past and present collide. Are you ready to face what you've buried?

She met his gaze, unwavering.

I'm ready.

The door creaked open, revealing a room filled with relics: old letters, photographs, and a worn journal—the key to everything.

As she picked up the journal, the labyrinth around them seemed to hold its breath.

The story was far from over.

She opened the journal with trembling hands. The pages were yellowed, the ink faded but still legible — a tapestry of secrets woven in careful script.

Each entry pulled her deeper into the life of the man she'd been chasing, revealing a world tangled in shadows and light.

There were confessions of lost love, coded messages hinting at hidden alliances, and cryptic references to places that didn't exist on any map.

One page caught her eye — a sketch of a door, identical to the one they had just crossed, but inscribed with a symbol she hadn't seen before: a key intertwined with a serpent.

Before she could ponder its meaning, the ground beneath them shifted. The labyrinth groaned, walls trembling as if alive.

The man beside her whispered, The deeper you go, the more the labyrinth tests you. The truth demands sacrifice.

She swallowed hard, knowing that with every revelation, the price of discovery grew heavier.

But there was no turning back now.

She closed the journal and looked up.

Show me the way.

The spiral pulsed once again, leading them onward — toward answers, and shadows yet unknown.

The corridor beyond the chamber stretched endlessly, walls alive with shifting patterns that seemed to pulse in rhythm with her heartbeat.

The symbol from the journal—the serpent entwined with the key—glowed faintly, guiding their steps.

Every twist revealed fragments of forgotten histories: whispers of a man who trafficked secrets like currency, shadows of betrayal that reached beyond time.

The air thickened, heavy with the weight of unspoken truths.

Her companion's voice broke the silence:

Not all labyrinths are built to trap. Some are made to protect.

She glanced at him, questions burning in her eyes.

Protect from what?

A past too dangerous to surface, he said. And a future too fragile to risk.

Ahead, a faint light flickered, and the scent of old paper and dust filled the air.

They arrived at a vast library carved into the stone—rows upon rows of books and manuscripts, each one a piece of the puzzle.

In the center, an ancient desk held a single locked box, sealed with the serpent-key symbol.

He handed her an ornate key, cold and heavy.

This is your choice. Open it, and the labyrinth reveals its deepest secret.

Her fingers closed around the key.

The moment the lock clicked, a new chapter began.

The box creaked open, releasing a faint, musty scent — a mixture of time and secrets long kept.

Inside lay a bundle of letters tied with a faded ribbon, and beneath them, a small, intricately carved amulet shaped like the serpent entwined with the key.

She unfolded the top letter, the handwriting trembling yet determined.

**To the one who finds this,

You carry more than bloodline—you carry the burden of choices made in shadows.

The man you seek was not only a trader of goods, but of fates. His actions carved paths for many, including you.

This labyrinth is his legacy—both prison and sanctuary.

Seek the heart where light and dark converge. There you will find what was lost, and what must never be found.

Her breath caught.

The amulet pulsed gently in her palm — a heartbeat echoing through stone and silence.

The labyrinth wasn't just a maze of walls and tunnels; it was a living story, a riddle waiting to be solved.

Her journey was no longer about uncovering the past — it was about shaping what came next.

She met his eyes, steady and knowing.

Let's find the heart.

Together, they stepped deeper into the mystery — where every shadow held a truth, and every truth demanded courage.

The deeper they ventured, the colder the air grew, thickening with whispers only half-heard. Flickering torches lined the walls, their flames struggling against an unseen breath that seemed to move with the labyrinth itself.

At every turn, symbols like the serpent and key reappeared — etched into stone, painted faintly on crumbling walls, carved into the handles of ancient doors. They weren't just markers; they were warnings.

Suddenly, a distant sound echoed—a soft, rhythmic tapping, like footsteps or a heartbeat. They followed it, descending a spiral staircase that wound downward into darkness.

At the bottom, the passage opened into a cavernous chamber, where a pool of black water mirrored the flickering torchlight. In the center, a pedestal held an ancient book bound in worn leather.

As she approached, the surface of the water rippled, revealing fleeting images—faces, places, memories—that seemed both foreign and intimately familiar.

Her hand hovered over the book.

Are you ready? he asked.

She nodded.

Opening the book, the air shifted, and the labyrinth seemed to pulse in response.

The journey was far from over.

As the pages turned, the ink seemed to breathe—words shifting, revealing secrets written in languages both ancient and strange.

Images flickered within the text: a man cloaked in shadow, a woman with eyes like storms, a labyrinth stretching beyond the edges of the known world.

Her fingers traced a map hidden within the margins, lines connecting forgotten places and whispered names.

The heart, she whispered. It's not just a place. It's a choice.

Behind her, the sound of footsteps grew closer—slow, deliberate, deliberate enough to chill the spine.

Someone's here, he murmured, reaching for a hidden dagger.

The shadows lengthened.

A voice emerged from the darkness—a voice that carried both threat and promise.

You seek what was lost. But are you ready for what will be found.

The labyrinth held its breath.

And so did they.

The voice was closer now—echoing off the stone walls, wrapping around them like a shroud.

From the darkness emerged a figure, cloaked, but with eyes that gleamed like embers in the firelight.

I've walked these tunnels longer than you can imagine, the stranger said, voice low and steady. The man you seek left more than shadows behind. He left a legacy tangled in danger and desire.

She stepped forward, heart pounding. Tell us what we need to know.

The figure nodded slowly, producing a folded parchment from inside their cloak.

This map leads to the core of the labyrinth — the place where truth and nightmare collide. But beware—the path demands sacrifice, and the price is never paid in coin.

He handed her the map.

A cold breeze swept through the chamber, stirring t ancient dust, carrying with it the scent of forgotten promises.

The labyrinth awaited, and time was running thin.

Are you ready to cross the line? The stranger asked.

She met his gaze, steady as steel.

Yes.

Together they stepped forward.

The map glowed faintly under her touch, the lines shifting as if alive—guiding them deeper, further than they'd dared before.

Each step forward drew whispers from the walls, voices half-remembered, warnings half-forgotten.

At a fork, the path split into two: one narrow and dark, the other wide but lined with statues whose eyes seemed to follow their every move.

Which way? he asked, tension taut in his voice.

She studied the map. The narrow path pulsed with a soft red glow—danger. The wider path, a cold blue—mystery.

Both, she decided. We split. It's the only way.

They exchanged a glance—trust forged in fire—and parted ways into the shadows.

Alone, the labyrinth seemed to close in, breathing around her, testing her will.

Somewhere ahead, a secret waited — one that could unravel everything, or save it all.

Her footsteps echoed softly as she pressed forward down the narrow path, the red glow pulsing faintly beneath the cracked stones. Every breath felt heavier, the air thick with a sense of unseen eyes watching, waiting.

Suddenly, a low hum filled the space — like a heartbeat, steady and unyielding. The walls seemed to pulse in rhythm, guiding her deeper into the labyrinth's core.

Ahead, a door carved with the same serpent symbol as before stood slightly ajar. Beyond it, faint light flickered—warm, inviting, but tinged with something else: warning.

She reached out, fingers trembling, and pushed the door open.

Inside, an old workshop stretched before her — dust-covered canvases, broken brushes, and sketches pinned to the walls. In the center, a portrait stood on an easel — the man from the picture in her mother's purse. His eyes seemed to follow her, alive with a secret only half-spoken.

A folded letter lay tucked beneath the frame. She unfolded it carefully:

To the one who finds this — the labyrinth is more than stone and shadow. It is a test of truth, a mirror

to the soul. The path we walk is never straight, but in the twists and turns, you will find yourself. Seek the light, even when darkness beckons.

Her breath caught.

Behind her, footsteps approached — slow, deliberate, and no longer alone.

She spun around, heart pounding, ready to face whoever stepped through the threshold. But the figure that appeared was not what she expected — it was the painter himself, or at least his echo, aged and worn like a ghost trapped between worlds.

His eyes held both sorrow and urgency.

You've come far, he said, voice trembling like a forgotten song. But the labyrinth isn't just a maze of stone. It's a web of choices, lies, and forgotten ties. Your father—he vanished here because he sought to break the cycle. To find freedom.

She clenched the letter tighter, feeling the weight of the mystery settle deeper.

Why did he disappear? She whispered

The painter's gaze darkened.

Because some truths are more dangerous than shadows. The mafia, the traders, the secrets they buried—they all lead here. To the heart of the labyrinth. And to the face you saw once. The face that can either save you, or consume you.

He stepped back into the shadows, fading as the door creaked open behind him.

From the darkness came a whisper, chilling and clear:

Choose wisely. The labyrinth watches.

She folded the letter, took a deep breath, and stepped into the unknown once more.

The air grew colder as she moved past the fading figure, the whisper lingering like a ghost on her skin. Every step echoed louder, the labyrinth's pulse quickening, as if sensing her resolve — or her doubt.

Her phone vibrated sharply in her pocket. A message from the friend waiting at the other path:

Found something. Meet at the center. Urgent.

The path ahead twisted, walls narrowing. Shadows lengthened, threatening to swallow the light.

She swallowed her fear, clutching the letter like a talisman.

The labyrinth wasn't just a maze of stone—it was a battleground of secrets, and the next choice would define everything.

Ahead, the spiral carved into the floor glowed faintly, the pattern alive and shifting — calling her forward.

She stepped onto it.

The ground beneath her feet seemed to dissolve, the spiral's glow wrapping around her ankles like liquid fire. The walls melted into darkness, and for a moment, she felt suspended—between time, between reality, between what was and what might be.

When her vision cleared, she was somewhere else. A room bathed in flickering candlelight, heavy with the scent of old paper and forgotten secrets.

In the center, a table was strewn with maps, letters, and photographs—fragments of a life half-lived and stories half-told.

She reached out and picked up a faded photograph: her mother, younger, smiling softly beside a man whose face was both familiar and foreign—the man in the purse.

A sudden noise—a soft scrape behind her—made her spin.

The door creaked open slowly, and there stood the woman from the café in Prague, eyes shadowed but steady.

We don't have much time, she said. The labyrinth is shifting. And so are the players. Your father's secrets are deeper than we imagined.

The walls seemed to pulse again.

She nodded, heart racing. "What do we do now?"

The woman stepped inside, closing the door behind her. We follow the threads—the hidden paths beneath the city. The tunnels where deals were made, and promises broken.

A soft rumble echoed through the floor, as if the labyrinth itself was awakening.

Your father's past isn't just history, the woman whispered. It's a map. And if we read it right, it could lead us to the truth—or to danger we're not prepared for.

She pulled out a worn key, its metal etched with strange symbols. This opens the first gate. After that, the labyrinth chooses who stays—and who disappears.

The candlelight flickered violently.

There was no turning back.

Together, they stepped toward the hidden door, the shadows folding around them like a cloak.

She nodded, heart racing. What do we do now?

The woman stepped inside, closing the door behind her. "We follow the threads—the hidden paths beneath the city. The tunnels where deals were made, and promises broken.

A soft rumble echoed through the floor, as if the labyrinth itself was awakening.

Your father's past isn't just history, the woman whispered. It's a map. And if we read it right, it could lead us to the truth—or to danger we're not prepared for.

She pulled out a worn key, its metal etched with strange symbols. This opens the first gate. After that, the labyrinth chooses who stays—and who disappears.

The candlelight flickered violently.

There was no turning back.

Together, they stepped toward the hidden door, the shadows folding around them like a cloak.

The hidden door groaned as it swung open, revealing a narrow staircase descending into cold darkness. The air smelled of damp stone and forgotten years.

With only a flicker of candlelight to guide them, they began their descent. Every step echoed — a reminder that they were not alone.

Halfway down, a faint scratch traced along the wall, like a message left in haste.

She paused, tracing the marks with trembling fingers.

Symbols—ancient, cryptic—wove a warning: Trust none but the spiral.

Her companion's eyes met hers, a flicker of fear hidden beneath steel resolve.

The labyrinth was more than a place. It was a living enigma.

And the deeper they went, the closer they drew to the heart of the unknown.

The staircase ended abruptly in a cavernous chamber, the walls lined with flickering torches that revealed intricate frescoes—stories of betrayal, sacrifice, and redemption.

In the center stood a pedestal, holding an ancient book bound in cracked leather, its pages yellowed with age.

She reached out, fingers trembling, and opened it.

The script inside was not written in any language she knew, but the spiral symbol repeated on every page seemed to pulse with life.

A sudden chill swept through the room as a voice whispered from the shadows:

Every labyrinth has its guardian. Are you ready to face yours?

The flickering torches dimmed.

Darkness stretched out.

From the shadows emerged a figure—tall, cloaked, face hidden beneath a hood.

His presence was both menacing and oddly familiar, like a ghost from a forgotten past.

You seek answers, he said, voice low and gravelly. But every truth demands a price.

She swallowed hard. I'm ready.

He stepped forward, extending a hand holding a small, ornate key — identical to the one she had seen before.

This opens the final door, the one your father never dared cross. Beyond it lies the secret that could change everything.

The spiral on the floor glowed brighter, drawing them closer to the threshold.

With a deep breath, she took the key.

The moment of reckoning had arrived.

She felt the weight of the key in her palm, cold and heavy—like a fragment of a past she barely understood but couldn't ignore.

The cloaked figure stepped aside, revealing an ancient door carved deep into the stone wall. The spiral motif curled around the edges, glowing faintly in the dim light.

Her fingers trembled as she inserted the key into the lock. A slow, grinding sound echoed through the chamber as the door began to open, revealing a narrow passage shrouded in shadows.

With every step forward, the air grew thicker, charged with secrets and unseen eyes.

Then, suddenly, the passage opened into a vast underground hall.

There, in the center, stood a solitary figure — a man whose face was both familiar and strange.

The face she had seen once.

And the journey to uncover the truth was only just beginning.

The man's eyes locked onto hers — a mixture of recognition and something darker, unreadable.

He stepped forward slowly, his voice low but steady.

I never wanted you to find this place. Some truths are buried for a reason.

Her heart pounded. Who are you? Why did my mother keep your picture all these years?

A bitter smile crossed his lips. I'm the shadow in your family's story. The man they warned you about. But also the key to what was lost.

Behind him, the labyrinth walls seemed to pulse, alive with whispers and memories.

You want answers. You'll need to face the maze inside yourself first.

He held out a small box, worn but ornate.

Inside this lies your inheritance. But beware — the past doesn't forgive easily.

She reached for the box, feeling the weight of generations resting in her hands.

The labyrinth was no longer just a place. It was a legacy. And it demanded everything.

She opened the box with trembling hands. Inside lay a delicate, ancient pendant—its center a swirling spiral, catching the faint torchlight like a living thing.

As she touched it, visions flashed behind her closed eyes: a crowded London street, whispered conversations in shadowed alleyways, secret meetings, betrayals, and a father she never truly knew.

The man's voice broke through the flood of images.

That spiral is more than a symbol. It's a map—of places, people, choices. It binds you to the labyrinth and to him.

Her breath caught. To him.

He nodded.

The man from your mother's purse. The one you've been chasing. He left this behind, hoping someone—you, would find the way through the darkness.

The chamber seemed to breathe with anticipation.

Are you ready to step deeper, or will you turn back into the light of forgotten truths.

The labyrinth was waiting, its mystery unfolding, one step closer to the heart of everything.

She clutched the pendant tighter, its spiral seeming to pulse in rhythm with her heartbeat.

I'm ready, she said, voice steady despite the storm inside.

The man nodded solemnly. Then follow me.

He led her through a narrow archway, descending deeper into the labyrinth's bowels—where shadows stretched longer, and silence was thick with secrets.

The walls were etched with symbols—ancient scripts weaving stories of loss, power, and forbidden knowledge.

Each mark, he explained, is a clue left by those who came before, trapped between hope and despair.

Suddenly, the path split into two — one side bathed in faint, cold blue light, the other swallowed by darkness.

The choice, he said, is yours. The blue path reveals truth but demands sacrifice. The dark path hides secrets but may lead to ruin.

She hesitated, the pendant warm against her skin, urging her forward.

Her journey wasn't just through the labyrinth—it was through herself.

And the next step could change everything.

She took a deep breath, stepping toward the blue light. It was cold, almost biting, but clearer — like truth itself, sharp and unyielding.

With each step, the symbols on the walls seemed to glow, whispering forgotten names and warnings in a language she almost understood.

The man walked silently beside her, a shadow of his own past trailing behind.

Then, suddenly, the passage opened into a vast chamber.

At its center, an ancient pedestal held a cracked mirror, its surface swirling like liquid night.

This, he said, is the Reflection of Lost Time. It shows what was, what is, and what might have been.

She stepped closer, heart pounding.

As her fingers brushed the mirror, the surface rippled—and her own face stared back, but not alone.

Behind her, flickering shadows moved—faces she recognized and others she didn't, all tangled in a story she was only beginning to unravel.

The labyrinth wasn't just a maze of stone—it was a mirror of souls, of secrets waiting to be faced.

Are you ready to look deeper? the man asked, his voice barely a whisper.

She hesitated, eyes locked on the shifting faces within the mirror's depths. Each one told a story—loss, betrayal, hope—threads of a past tangled with her own.

I have to, she whispered, voice trembling.

The moment she stepped fully into the reflection, the chamber seemed to dissolve, replaced by a whirlwind of memories not her own—fragments of a man's life she never knew, yet somehow felt connected to.

She saw the man from London—her possible father—moving through shadowed streets, trading secrets with dangerous men, haunted by choices he couldn't undo.

But then, a sudden flash: a hidden door within the labyrinth, marked by the same spiral as the pendant.

This is where he vanished, the man's voice echoed beside her.

Her heart surged. The labyrinth's mystery was no longer just a puzzle—it was a living story waiting for her to finish.

She knew what she had to do next.

Step beyond the mirror.

Step into the unknown.

With a steadying breath, she reached forward—and the mirror's surface rippled like water, parting before her like a doorway.

Stepping through, the world shifted. Cold stone walls replaced the shimmering light, and the distant echo of dripping water filled the air.

Before her stretched a narrow tunnel, carved deep beneath the city—dark, winding, alive.

The spiral on her pendant glowed faintly, guiding her steps.

Behind, the man's footsteps echoed softly, a reminder she wasn't alone.

Each step drew her closer to the truth hidden in shadows—her father's past, the secrets buried in the labyrinth, and a destiny tangled in fear, sacrifice, and hope.

The path was uncertain, but she knew this journey was hers alone to walk.

And somewhere ahead, the labyrinth waited—ready to reveal what had long been lost.

Into the tunnel's depths she moved, the air growing heavier with each step. Faint inscriptions lined the walls — symbols half-erased by time, whispering of forgotten rites and warnings.

The pendant pulsed softly, a heartbeat syncing with hers, pulling her forward.

Suddenly, the path split — two corridors, both cloaked in shadows.

A cold breeze drifted from the left, carrying a scent of damp earth and something else — faint, metallic, like old blood.

The right corridor hummed with a low vibration, as if the stone itself was alive beneath her feet.

The man looked to her, eyes steady.

Which way leads to the truth? he asked.

Her fingers tightened around the pendant.

This way, she said, stepping toward the left — toward the dark, uncertain path where the labyrinth's secrets whispered loudest.

The cold breeze wrapped around her like a warning, but she pressed forward, each footfall swallowed by the thick silence. The tunnel walls seemed to close in, the faded symbols now sharper, glowing faintly with an ancient light. They told a story—a story of betrayal, sacrifice, and a hidden legacy.

A distant sound echoed—a faint scraping, like claws against stone. Her heart hammered as the pendant's pulse quickened.

Suddenly, a figure stepped from the shadows—the man from the portrait, or someone bearing his likeness—eyes sharp, unreadable.

You shouldn't be here," he said, voice low and gravelly. "This labyrinth doesn't forgive trespassers.

Her grip tightened on the pendant. I'm not leaving without answers.

He studied her, then nodded slowly.

Then you must face the darkness within, and the truth beneath.

The labyrinth had awakened—and so had the secrets buried deep inside.

The man stepped aside, revealing a narrow spiral staircase winding down into the abyss. The air grew colder, thick with the weight of untold stories and forgotten sins.

You'll need more than courage, he warned. This path tests more than your resolve—it will strip you bare, forcing you to confront what you hide even from yourself.

She glanced at the pendant, now glowing steadily, as if fueling her will.

With a final breath, she descended.

Each step echoed like a heartbeat in the hollow dark, shadows twisting into shapes—whispers of the past clawing at her mind.

At the bottom, a heavy iron door awaited, carved with the spiral emblem.

Her hand trembled as she pushed it open.

Beyond lay the chamber where the past and present collided—the place where her father's story, the painter's secrets, and the labyrinth's curse would finally intertwine.

The truth was waiting. And this time, she was ready.

The chamber was vast, its walls draped in fading tapestries that seemed to breathe with history. At the center stood an ornate pedestal, cradling a weathered journal bound in cracked leather.

She approached, heart pounding, the pendant now a steady glow lighting the room's edges.

Opening the journal, she found pages filled with cryptic sketches, fragmented letters, and a single phrase repeated in looping script: The face I saw once holds the key.

A sudden noise — the scraping sound again — drew her gaze to a shadow moving near the far wall.

The man from London stepped forward, face grim.

This is where it begins, he said. The past you chase is more than memory. It's a choice—and a burden.

She met his eyes, feeling the weight of the labyrinth settle deep in her bones.

We either unravel it here... or remain lost forever.

The air thickened with tension as the two stood facing each other, shadows dancing in the dim light.

Why did you disappear? she asked quietly. Why leave it all behind?

He looked away, pain flickering in his eyes. Because some truths are too dangerous—too heavy for one person to carry.

She stepped closer, the journal clasped tight in her hands. But the labyrinth brought me here for a reason. To finish what was started.

He nodded slowly. Then we're bound by the same thread — yours, mine, and hers. He gestured toward the journal. The painter, your father, the labyrinth... it's all connected.

A sudden rumble shook the chamber. Dust fell from the ceiling as ancient mechanisms creaked to life.

The labyrinth isn't done with us yet, he warned.

Together, they prepared to delve deeper — into the heart of the maze, where the final secret waited, cloaked in shadows and bloodlines.

And with every step, the past grew closer — ready to either claim them or set them free.

The walls began to shift, slow but deliberate—ancient gears turning beneath the stone, revealing a narrow passage bathed in a cold, pale light.

She glanced at the man. No turning back now.

He gave a grim nod. This path was hidden for a reason. What we find may change everything we thought we knew.

They stepped forward together, the air growing heavier with each breath, as whispers from long ago curled around them like smoke.

The passage opened into a cavern, where flickering torches cast jagged shadows on relics half-buried in dust — relics of a life erased.

On the far side, a mural stretched across the wall: a story told in blood-red and gold — a father, a painter, a labyrinth, and a face that kept appearing, watching.

She traced the lines with her fingers, feeling the weight of history settle deeper inside.

This is the beginning of the end, she whispered.

And somewhere, deep in the maze, a silent voice answered.

A faint breeze stirred the stagnant air, carrying with it a scent of earth and forgotten secrets.

The man reached out, revealing a small, rusted key — one she hadn't noticed before, tucked inside his coat.

This, he said, opens the door behind the mural.

Heart pounding, she stepped forward. The stone surface shifted under her touch, revealing a hidden doorway carved into the rock.

They crossed the threshold into darkness, their footsteps echoing against cold stone walls etched with symbols older than memory.

Ahead, a faint glow pulsed — like the heartbeat of the labyrinth itself.

As they moved closer, the glow revealed a glass case holding a single object: a faded portrait of the man from her mother's purse.

But the eyes — they seemed alive, watching, waiting.

The labyrinth had finally unveiled its deepest secret.

And the face she saw once was no longer just a memory.

It was a beginning.

The portrait's eyes seemed to burn with a silent warning — a banishment not just to her, but to many who had dared to seek the truth.

A voice echoed softly in the chamber, half-remembered and half-feared:

The deeper you delve, the darker the maze becomes. The more you fear, the further you descend into shadow.

She swallowed hard, the weight of that warning settling like a stone in her chest.

But the pull was irresistible — the labyrinth wasn't just a prison of fear; it was a forge.

And only by facing the darkness head-on could they hope to find the light waiting at its heart.

To bring the light, they had to carry the shadows within them—embrace the fear, the loss, the unknown.

The labyrinth was not just a maze of stone, but a mirror of the soul.

Each step forward was a confrontation with the parts of themselves they had long buried.

She tightened her grip on the portrait, feeling the weight of her past and the promise of a future intertwined.

Light isn't the absence of darkness, she whispered, it's what we create when we refuse to be consumed by it.

Together, they moved deeper, ready to face whatever waited — because only through the labyrinth's heart could the true path be revealed.

The walls around them seemed to pulse, alive with whispers of forgotten stories and hidden pain. Every shadow stretched longer, every corner concealed a secret. Yet, with each breath, the air grew lighter—an unseen force urging them onward.

She felt the portrait warm in her hands, as if responding to her courage. The man beside her glanced back, eyes sharp but softened by trust.

This labyrinth tests more than our steps, he said quietly. It tests what we're willing to face in ourselves.

Ahead, a faint glow flickered — not harsh or blinding, but steady, patient.

The light was waiting.

They stepped toward the glow, their shadows merging with the light, dissolving the space between fear and hope.

The path twisted, revealing fragments of memories — hers, his, and the labyrinth's own whispered past.

A sudden chill swept through, and the air thickened with the weight of untold stories.

Then, from the depths, a voice — neither threatening nor kind — spoke:

To find the truth, you must surrender what you think you know.

She hesitated, then let go.

In that moment, the labyrinth opened wider, the light blossomed, and the face she saw once stepped forward from the shadows — no longer a mystery, but a living thread weaving their fate.

The face was older now, lined with years of secrets and silent regrets. Eyes that held storms and calm seas all at once.

Why did you disappear? she asked, voice trembling.

He smiled faintly, shadows flickering in the glow. Because some truths demand sacrifice. Because the labyrinth is not just a place—it's a choice.

He stepped closer, the air thick with unspoken promises. You've come far, but the path ahead is yours to shape.

Her heart quickened. The maze, the man, the memories—they were all pieces of a puzzle that only now began to make sense.

Then I choose, she whispered, to walk forward — not as a lost soul, but as the one who carries the light.

He nodded slowly, as if the weight of her words lifted something long buried.

The labyrinth will test you still. It will challenge your fears, your doubts, even your very identity. But remember — every shadow you face is part of you. To conquer it, you must embrace it.

She felt the pulse of the place grow stronger, as if the walls themselves were alive, waiting for her next move.

Are you ready? he asked, eyes searching hers.

She took a deep breath, feeling the past, the mystery, the unknown all blend into a fierce resolve.

Yes. Because this time, I'm not running. I'm creating my own path.

And with that, the labyrinth seemed to breathe — opening wide, inviting her deeper into its heart, where the next secret waited, patient and alive.

The city outside awaited—alive with light and shadow, stories weaving endlessly through its streets.

You and your friend emerged from the labyrinth changed—carriers of truths both heavy and freeing.

The face she once saw wasn't just a memory anymore; it was a doorway to understanding, forgiveness, and new beginnings.

As you walked away from the Spiral's glow, the first rays of dawn painted the sky—soft, promising, and infinite.

And in that quiet morning, you knew:

Every ending is the seed of a new story.

Every face, no matter how briefly seen, leaves a mark that shapes who we become.

The labyrinth is never truly behind you—it turns within, guiding you forward.

The Face I Saw Once, is not just a story of mystery and loss.

It's a journey through the shadows we carry—and the light we choose to follow.

The Spiral turns.

And so, do we.

Acknowledgments

This story would not have come to life without the support and inspiration of many. To those who embrace the mysteries of life and the unknown roots that shape us—thank you for walking this labyrinth with me.

My deepest gratitude to my friends and family for their patience and belief, to the places that sparked imagination, and to the silent moments where stories whispered themselves into being.

To the readers who dare to explore hidden paths, may this journey resonate with your own search for light through darkness.

About the Author:

Zoe Vlamaki :(nick-name, Zoella) is the author of several previous works exploring consciousness, perception, and the hidden layers of human experience. With a distinctive voice that bridges poetic insight and philosophical depth, her writing continues to resonate with readers across generations.

List of books: by Zoe Vlamaki
The Beginning of Trust
The Truth Never Told
In my Roots Life Unfolds
Behind the White Wall
Life Cross the Borders
Unstoppable
Raising in the Light
The Blue stone
The Day of the Reflection
The Round Table
The Face I Saw Once

About the Author

Author: Zoella*About the Author*Zoe Vlamaki is a medical professional, writer, and human rights advocate with decades of experience working across cultures and continents. Her journey through different societies has shaped her deep understanding of identity, displacement, and the quiet strength of truth.Driven by a passion to give voice to untold stories, she writes with raw honesty and emotional depth. *The Truth Never Told* is her deeply personal reflection on silence, struggle, and the hidden lives of those often overlooked.She currently lives between Greece and the UK, continuing her work in medicine while dedicating her time to writing and advocacy.

Read more at www.biovitalyclinic.com.